TWINKLE

NATHAN A GOODMAN

THOUGHT REACH PRESS

THOUGHT REACH PRESS, a publishing division of Thought Reach, LLC. Atlanta, Georgia, United States of America

ISBN- 978-0-9905738-5-2

First Thought Reach Press printing August 2015

For information regarding special discounts for bulk purchases, or permission to reproduce any content other than mentioned above, contact the publisher at support@thoughtreach.com.

Printed in the USA

Other novels by Nathan A. Goodman:

The bestseller *The Fourteenth Protocol*, an FBI thriller. A tale of loss, corruption, and the power of the one.

To anyone who has ever questioned God.
To anyone who is still filled with questions.
And to those of us believers who carry on not knowing all the answers.

About fifteen years ago, out of the blue, I sat down and wrote the first page of what was to later become the novel Twinkle. I didn't know where the words came from. I wasn't really thinking about anything in particular when I was writing them, but there they were, spilling out onto the page. And that's where the story sat, for fifteen years. Then, all those years later, I was in the middle of writing a sequel to my novel *The Fourteenth Protocol*, and the story was really starting to take on a life of its own. Characters were forming, tension was building, and I was pleased because I had a lot of people asking when it would be released. But during this whole time, I kept looking over my shoulder. I was hearing something, something in the distance, something that wouldn't quiet, and it distracted me from my writing. It wasn't what you and I think of as a real sound though. It was more like a whisper, or the sound that might be heard when an oak leaf gives up its hold high above the forest floor, and floats gracefully to the ground. Despite my best intentions to ignore it, the sound wouldn't go away. It became frustrating. After all, I had a sequel brewing, and I was busy. But that's so much the story of our lives, isn't it? We fill our worlds with the busyness of our various concerns. It took me a long time to put my self-importance aside, and stop and listen to the sound. But finally, I got quiet. To do this I went on long walks and tried to flush everything else from my head, except for the sound. It still took me some time understand what the sound was. It was *Twinkle*. *Twinkle*, which hadn't even been put down on paper, was talking to me. For those of you that are not believers, this all sounds contrite. But those that are know what I'm talking about. The sound I was hearing was the sound of God breathing. He wasn't yelling. He wasn't angry with me. He just wanted me get quiet and listen to him long enough so he could tell me to pull *Twinkle* out of its hiding place deep within my heart, and let it breathe.

~*Nathan A. Goodman*

1
Into the Twinkle

On the little island of Saint Simons, not far from the pier, sits the public library, a larger building than one might imagine, and one that's eternally involved in the life of the small town. It sits just down from J.C. Strothers hardware store, and everybody on the island knows where that is. As the children gathered under some of the largest oak trees you've ever seen, an old man shuffled down the steps of the library and made his way up to the group. His skin was a beautiful mixed glow of pitch black and ebony. He found them all sitting criss-cross applesauce and waiting for the library's daily story time to begin. The live oak's branches were so large they swept down towards the ground and jutted out-wards like the tentacles of an octopus. When he sat his full weight down onto the oak branch, he didn't bother with introductions, but started right in. It was just his way, and the children liked him immediately.

"Did I ever tell you the story of the Magic Place? No? Oh, come on, now. I *know* someone had to tell you the Magic Place story. Everybody knows about... What? I never did tell it? Well, alright then, y'all all gather close and your old Mr. Winkles will tell y'all all about it." The old man gleamed at the circle of children and drew in a deep breath. "Way deep down south, in the windey, warm, waterway, stood a place of wonderment, joy, merriment, and magic. The Magic Place, they called it, for it was full of secrets, surprises, and magical mysteries.

"No grown up had ever been to the Magic Place, because to them, there was no magic left in the world. But to the children, the Magic Place was real, it was alive, and it was good. You see, they believed in it, and it believed in them. It thrived off their energy, their spirit, their laughter. And they thrived on its wonderment, joy, merriment, and magic. Did I mention the wonderment, joy, merriment, and magic already? Well, if I did, forgive me, because I be an old man who got but the spirit of a child left inside him. That little child that I used to be is gone, all growed up, but I still have just a bit of a little boy left in there, yessirree. Where was I? Oh yes, way deep down. Way deep down south. Because as long as I can remember the Magic Place, the Magic Place lives on.

"Now, I said that no grown ups believed in the Magic Place. That's because they never seen it. And even if they did see it, they couldn't believe in it, because most grown ups forget all the best parts of the wonderment, joy, merriment, and magic of being a child.

"Okay, now y'all scoot in a little bit. Y'all get closer together. Get closer to me. Slide all the way up to me and look down into the twinkle-winkle of my eye. No, you're too far away, you need to get closer to find the twinkle-winkle of a person's eye. Y'all ain't never heard of the twinkle-winkle? The twinkle-winkle is where the eye ends and the magic begins. Lean all the way in. You see it? You see your own reflection in my eye? Now look close in my eye at *your* reflection, and find your own eye in there. If you look hard enough, into the reflection of your own eye, you'll see your way down to the Magic Place. Keep looking, keep looking, good! Now that's it! Come on down, way deep down south. Come on inside to the windey, warm, waterway, for the Magic Place lies within."

2
The Newel Post

The slave's name was Washington. He stood tall, easily over six feet, and could mount a horse with a simple leap. And even though he had no formal education, the width of his broad shoulders bestowed nothing to the depths of his mind which worked like the cogs of a mechanized clock, turning out thoughts and answers and solutions. Washington's complexion was as dark as the coals of a campfire, yet he had a heart as pure as new-fallen snow. The combination produced a rare equity on a rice plantation. He was owned, just like the land was owned; he produced, just like the land produced, and yet he was trusted, something the land and its new rice fields had yet to earn.

The landowner, Graydon Moon, was taking quite a risk by investing considerable resources in the clearing of the land, and formation of dozens of rice fields, or paddies, all along his property on the Georgia coast. Graydon's education in England taught him nothing of such things. But inheriting this piece of land brought him home, and he was determined to make a success where his father had failed.

Graydon stood next to Washington as his stark opposite. Graydon had been given everything, Washington had to earn everything, which is to say, he could earn only one thing—trust— for he could never earn his freedom.

Sweat rolled from underneath Washington's dense hairline, and a drop tumbled through the air and splashed onto the side of the freshly carved wood. He had started with a thick piece of live oak, cut from the center of the tree. He worked the wood down, shaving it closer and closer into shape with a long draw-knife. Then he began etching away at it, first with the large wood chisel, then the smaller ones. He worked the tools back and forth, shaving tiny slivers from the block until it melded into the shape he held in his mind's eye.

The carving, once finished, would be used as the cap for the newel post—the central supporting pillar of the stair rail. And, since it was to figure so prominently in the foyer of the plantation house, Master Graydon Moon's wife, Ivy, was more than keen for it to be a showpiece. Washington knew he had to make it perfect, just the way he had drawn it for her three weeks prior. And even though the work was exacting, he didn't mind because he was kept company by the master's sevenf-year-old daughter who reveled at his craft. She was a wonderful child, and was the spitting image of her mother.

3
The Plantation

The children at once found themselves surrounded by a thick fog that cleared to reveal Mr. Winkles still seated in front of them. They hadn't moved from underneath the massive oak trees with their characteristic shapes and sweeping branches, but to each child it appeared that the trees were much smaller, younger. And gone was everything familiar including the library, park benches, sidewalks, the pier, and even J.C. Strothers hardware store. In fact, the children now appeared to be surrounded by nothing but nature. It was almost as though they had stepped back in time, and in fact, they had.

Mr. Winkles didn't even pause. "It was a long, long time ago..."

"Ah, Mr. Winkles?" said a little boy.

"Yes?"

"Is this the Magic Place right here?"

"Oh no, child. This ain't the Magic Place we're sitting in right here, but it's not far off. See, before you can understand the Magic Place, you've got to hear *this* story first. That's why I brought all of y'all here. Now, where was I? Oh yes. It was a long, long time ago. Way back in a dark time when some mammas and some papas and even some children were living way deep down south, living as slaves, working and working. Surviving and surviving. Living on plantations way deep down south. Living on plantations and working in the rice fields. Way deep down south. Waaaay back in the day. Way back before even your momma and your papa were born. Way down in the marshes, creeks, rivers, finger streams and them cypress forests. Waaaay deep down along the Georgia coast where the tide comes a long distance into the land. It comes all the way up in them bayous, creeks, rivers, and finger streams. Oh, I missed the marshes. Way up in them marshes too. Way down with all the life God created in the world. Way deep down with all the animals. The animals live together, talk together, laugh together, and play together in the Magic Place. They are bound together in this special place. Way deep down south.

"You see, children, to understand this story, you've got to understand that the world ain't always such a nice place. Even here, people used to think it was okay to have slaves. They thought that they were better. They thought the Bible said it was okay. They thought they were right. Well, they thought wrong.

"Hold on! Wait a minute. Get quiet children! Shhhh. Duck down over here behind them palmettos. Now listen, can y'all hear that? Don't let these folks see us. But if you listen close you can hear it. Way off over that'ta way. You can hear them singing. Slaves working on the rice fields. They're singing. Singing to pass the time. Singing to pass the day. Singing to get through all this hard work. Shhhh! Get down. Don't let them mean people see us. The mean people are the unhappy ones of this world. They are the ones who tell the slaves what to do. Those people are called *drivers*. But just listen to that sweeeet music."

"....swing low....sweet chaaaaariooooottt, comin' forth to carry me home....."

"Stay quiet children. Lets sneak over there. Keep your heads down low. I think I see Jupiter. Jupiter's a little boy about your age that I want to tell you about. He's my friend. He's out here working with the men. He brings them water and runs to get things when the mean driver-men want something. His daddy is named Washington, and he's one of the slaves too, building another rice field with the men. They work down here in the marsh. Down here in the windey, warm, waterway digging out the marsh. Digging and digging. Making walls out of mud and logs and rocks, all around for the rice field. Making walls...well, we call them kinds of walls *dikes*, so water can be held in there to grow the rice. It's hard work, back-breaking work. They cut down all the trees and palmettos and drag them outta the marsh, making room for the rice field.

"And them mosquitoes! Mosquitoes is everywhere down here in the marsh. Way deep down south. The mosquitoes are as big as birds! Well, not really big as birds. But big anyway! You've got to watch out for them gators too. There are some big ones in these marshes and finger creeks. Every once in a while, one of them takes down one of the men. Down into the water. Down into the darkness. The poor soul never to be heard from again.

"Now all this here story I be telling y'all and showing y'all happened long time ago. Long, long time ago, that's for sure. But the story started because of kids just like you all. Yeah, I know, y'all been getting into mischief, ain't ya? He-he-he. Well, that's okay; everybody gets into some mischief now and again, yessirree. Okay, so where was I? Oh, yeah, I was saying that all this here started when some kids got into some mischief. Anybody gonna guess who started it?"

Several children raised their hands and waved frantically at Mr. Winkles.

"Now, how about you? What about you, there, little man? You ain't got your hand a raised like all these other children. Come on over here and sit on old Mr. Winkles' lap. Now, don't be shy none. You know Mr. Winkles not gonna bite ya, right?"

The little boy looked as though he was about to sit on the scorching-hot vinyl in the backseat of an old station wagon but glanced at the other children who seemed unencumbered around Mr. Winkles.

"That's it, good. Just have a seat right here. Now, what's your name?"

"Leonard," said the small tike. "But I like to go by Lenny."

"Well then, Lenny, what you think, eh? Who do you think is about to cause the mischief?"

"Well," said the little boy, "must be that boy Jupiter over there. He's the only one around here."

"And you just right as rain! Just as right as rain! Jupiter was one of them little rascals that got this whole thing started in the first place. But, he didn't do it alone, did he? Let me ask y'all a question. Do y'all usually get into trouble all by your lonesome? Or when it happens, does you usually have a friend with ya?" He looked down at Lenny.

"Well, lemme think," said Lenny. "I supposed I get into much of my trouble when I'm with a friend."

"That's right. Right as rain. Mmm, mmm, mmm. You is a bit smarter than you give yourself credit for, Meestah Lenny, that's for sure. Alright, now. Jupiter over there is really just like you children. He grew up way back here during the slave days, but he ain't no different than you. He's a kid, and kids is kids is kids. Ain't that right? Yeah, y'all know it is. So lets all wander over yonder. Come on now, everybody follow me. We're gonna walk up this here path through those palmettos and cattails and stuff, sure as you're born, we is. We'll go up and see us a pretty girl. Now y'all just follow me. We gonna find a great big plantation house right up yonder. Hey that's it! Y'all can see it? All shaded under the great big oaks. Good, now gather round and we gonna...oh wait! Everybody duck! Duck down! Don't let her see ya! Now hush. Shhhh. Y'all all get quiet. That's her! That's the one I was fixing to tell y'all about. Hey, Lenny, get on up here boy. I got to show you the prettiest little girl ever was down here on Saint Simons Island. Now just take a look at that and tell me she ain't the prettiest little thing you ever done seen."

"You sure are right, sir," said Lenny, his eyes gaping. "She's like, she's like, she's like an angel."

"Y'all can call me *Mr. Winkles*, you got that Lenny?" laughed Winkles. "An angel, huh? An angel. Well, hmmm. Let me figure on that a minute. Hmmm, an angel. Well, Lenny, it's kind of funny you should say that. Kind of funny indeed. An angel."

"Why is it funny, Mr. Winkles?"

"Oh, we'll get to that, we'll get to it Lenny."

The girl didn't bother using the steps that lead down from the high porch, but instead leapt down onto a pile of live oak leaves she had scooped together the previous day. Her golden, feather-weight hair wafted upwards in the process, and the bright colored hem of her dress poofed into a parachute-like shape as it caught the air. The thick leaves were brown from a year of lingering under the shrubs, yet still retained their curved and hardened shape. They crunched and splashed under the tromp of her feet, .

"Say, Lenny," said Mr. Winkles, "she's just about your age, ain't she?"

"Oh no, Mr. Winkles, I'm just seven. That angel there, she's got to be at least ten. She's a big girl."

Mr. Winkles leaned back and laughed, "She's a biggun, huh? Well, ain't that something. The boy says she's ten. Sure as you're born, he done, sure as you're born."

Mr. Winkles and the children remained crouched behind the thicket of palmettos and watched the little girl jump up and down on the pile of leaves.

Little Lenny was awe-struck, "Mr. Winkles, what's her name?" His words seemed to roll off his tongue without aid of his mind.

"Well that's Remmie!" he said, "That's Remmie, that is. Now y'all all lean in here just a bit. And keep ya heads down behind these here palmettos. Shhh, good, good." He leaned towards the children and brought his voice down to just a whisper. "Y'all remember Jupiter we saw a minute ago, just a bit back that way? Well, Jupiter and Remmie are best of friends, they are, best of friends."

The little girl skipped down the same path that the children and Mr. Winkles had just traversed.

"Jupiter!" she said, "Jupiter, let me help you with that water bucket." After years of her father's best efforts, Remmie's speech had slowly begun to curtail the accent of pure coastal Georgia. "Now you know it's too heavy."

"Remmie, no!" said the small slave boy, "We'll get into trouble. You know they don't like us playin' together none."

"Oh, you just hush," she said. "I'll help you with it till we get down to near the creek bed."

Jupiter pulled against the grip of her fingers on the wooden bucket handle, "Remmie, no. Them drivers gonna be mad at us. Them drivers don't like no white child playin' with no Gullah."

Lenny couldn't contain his question. "Mr. Winkles, what's a Gullah?"

"Hush now child." But he didn't mean it as a rebuke. "Shhh. We be talking about them Gullah's in a little bit."

Remmie pried his hand free, "Just you hush up little mister Jupiter. Named after a planet, you were. That means you're bound for something great. And those drivers aren't going to have any say about it." The warmth of her smile was disarming, and needled itself in between his fear, and the last vestige of his resistance.

4
The Spirit of the Eyes

"Mr. Winkles," said Lenny, tugging at a cloth patch sewn into the bottom edge of his gray sweater, "what's a Gullah? I never heard of a Gullah."

"Oooh," said Mr. Winkles, "well now, let's see. None of y'all ever heard tale of no Gullah?" The children looked at one another as if for approval, then shook their heads in unison. "Well then, let's see. Hmmm, well see, the way the story of the Gullah's been passed down from my momma, from her momma, from her momma, was that there was this people. They were called the Gullah's and they were living over in Africa. In a place over on the West side of Africa that folks used to call the Rice Coast. And they were real good at growing rice and making great food. But best of all they were known for being the best story tellers. And to this very day, there's a lot of them living near all these places like Saint Simons Island." Mr. Winkles put his finger in the corner of his mouth and stared off to the side, perhaps searching for the right words. "And, well, this ain't such a nice thing to tell, but, you kids got to know, yessirree, you kids got to know. Alright then, y'all all circle up right around here." The grandfatherly man waved his hands in a wide motion. "That's it, y'all all gather in a circle, just like we did when we were all back at the big oak trees out in front of the library, and let's all sit down, criss-cross applesauce-like. Good, good. Everybody got a good spot? Yeah y'all all do, sure as you're born. The Gullah people, huh? Well, like I was saying, there was this whole bunch of people living over in Africa. And since they were so good at growing rice, there were people over here in America that wanted them to come grow rice here. Well, the Gullah people got caught by some of their enemies. Well, the enemies had hold of them, see? And what the enemies did is they sold the Gullah people to some bad men who took them to America, bad men indeed."

Winkles felt his sweater being tugged again. "Mr. Winkles? Um, what do you mean, bad men?"

"Oh, well, children," said Winkles, "see, they're folks in this world that ain't good. Ain't good at all, nossirree. Just as sure as you're born, they ain't no good. And folks like that took all those Gullah people and put them on ships and sailed them over here. Those ships used to come right down here to these, what we call, *Golden Isles*, like right here on Saint Simons Island, yessirree."

"Are we still on Saint Simons Island, Mr. Winkles?"

"We sure are, but we are on it the way it used to be, way back in the day. We're back in the 1800's."

"Okay," said the boy. "But why did they take them from their homes? Just because they were good at growing rice?" His mouth formed a straight line; it was unclear if it was about to turn down or up.

Winkles picked Lenny up and put him on his lap with the gentleness of one setting an egg onto a plate, leaned close to his face, then put one solitary finger on Lenny's little nose. "I know, I know, Lenny." It was almost a whisper. "But don't you worry none. Don't you worry. Okay, so, where was I? Oh yeah, we were talking about the Gullahs. So, there are some bad men in the world, and those bad men took the Gullah people, and because they were so good at growing rice, they brought them right here to Saint Simons Island. And the Gullahs lived here and worked here...as *slaves*." He paused to survey the tiny faces. "That's right, just as sure as you're born, they were slaves, and they worked here growing the rice, and they lived here, and died here. Now all this happened long, long time ago. And that's what I brought you here to see. And there's some things about these folks I want you to see."

"Like what?"

"Well, in order to understand the Gullah people, and this here Magic Place story, you've got to understand what they are like, on the inside. You've got to know how they think, and where their true love is."

"But how do we see that?"

"Y'all take a look over there. See right over there by the river's edge? Well that's Jupiter's daddy, Washington. And he and Jupiter, and all these other men are slaves. Right now, they're diggin' out a big old place here in the marsh to make another rice field where they're gonna plant the rice. But what I want y'all to see is, if you look close enough, is something special in their eyes. Y'all see it? Stand up and look for yourself. Look down deep into their eyes."

"I can see their eyes, Mr. Winkles! I can see them!" said Lenny, but the pitch of his voice faltered, like a balloon giving up air. "But I don't know what I'm looking for. Hey, wait a minute. If we look deep into their eyes, are we gonna be whooshed away to some other place like when we looked into yours?"

The old man rocked backwards laughing, "No, no, Lenny. You ain't gonna go wooshin' nowhere else, sure as you're born. Well, if you look deep in their eyes, you can see something—something like a *spirit* in them. Something like they just know that they're gonna be okay. Like they know that one day, they're gonna be in heaven, and everything will be just fine."

Lenny gaped at the men working, "They're going to heaven?" His mouth hung open. "Wow wee."

"Sure as you're born, Meestah Lenny, sure as you're born. Now, there is a reason that these here men just know they are goin' to heaven. And it's got to do with an old legend of the Gullah people. See, these Gullah people had some old kin-folk that were here long, long ago. These kin-folk, well, they'd been brought over here from Africa about a hundred years earlier, and they were all slaves too. One day, they all got up and decided they're gonna show them slave drivers a thing or two. Yes they did, yessirree."

"What did they do, whatdidtheydo?" begged Lenny, as his hands patted up and down on his lap.

"Well Meestah Lenny, sir, I'm gonna tell you just what they did," tickling the boy in the ribs with a finger. Everybody lean in. Good, good. Y'all lean in close now." Mr. Winkles looked in all directions like a person about to tell a secret. "What I'm about to tell y'all is an old Saint Simons Island legend. See, we're sitting here on the banks of what they call Dunbar Creek. Well, as the legend goes, one day, right on this very spot, right here at Dunbar Creek, the kin-folk of the Gullah people just got up and walked out onto that water out there." He said it with the confidence of a witness.

Lenny arched up, "They did? They walked on the water?"

"Just as sure as you're born! They walked out on that water, then walked clear cross the ocean and went all the way back to their home in Africa, they did."

The children exchanged smiles and wide-eyed gapes.

"Anyway, when all the other slaves all around these islands heard tell of them kin-folk walking across the water back to Africa, they all got real proud inside. That's right, yessirree, they got real proud inside, and that pride, that *hope*," Winkles paused and looked deep into the children's eyes, "that's what you're seeing in these men's eyes right down here." He pointed and stood up with a little bounce in his feet. "That pride got passed all the way down to these Gullah people right here. That's pride, and that's more than pride," he said, "that's what it looks like when you are a person that knows you're going to heaven one day."

"Mr. Winkles, Mr. Winkles," tugged Lenny, "but, but, but, how did they do it? How did they walk across the water?"

"Well you just hang on there little Meestah, I'm gonna tell you. See children, we aren't normally walking on water, are we? No, no. We aren't. So how did they do it? Well, legend says the kin-folk didn't do it all on their own. Some folks say it was magic. But it was a little more than that. It wasn't just magic, no. The kin-folk of the Gullah people had the blessing of the Holy Spirit on them, yes they did. And with that Holy Spirit, y'all can do anything. Just as sure as you're born." He looked down at Lenny. "You understand now?"

Lenny pursed his lips together as if he'd bitten into a sour grape. "There's something I still don't understand. Why, why, why did those bad men bring them over here in the first place? That was mean, and it seems like the Holy Spirit has a lot to do already, without having to help a whole mess of people walk clear across the ocean."

Mr. Winkles roared with laughter, and his soft belly jiggled up and down. "You sure are a smart one. Aren't you, Meestah Lenny, yessirree. Well, now here's the thing. The mean people, well see, they all used to want slaves because having a whole mess of slaves used to make a man rich. Yessirree. The slaves would plant the rice or cotton or whatever they were planting, and the owner of the slaves would get all the money from the sale of the crops. Yessirree." Mr. Winkles stopped and spun around to his left with dexterity uncharacteristic for such an old man. He peered across the top of the palmetto outcropping, "Shhhh, y'all get down! Here they come, here they come."

Remmie and Jupiter walked up the trail that led from the river bank and shuffled quietly towards the woods. Remmie stayed concealed behind a long row of palmetto bushes by crouching low and waddling forward. She looked like a squat-low turtle. The effect served to hide her from the view of the drivers who were hovering over the men as they fought to remove a hickory stump from the ground.

"Remmie!" said Jupiter, "Remmie, stay down."

Remmie waddled forward, moving almost as fast as a person walking upright. "Oh, you worry too much for someone named for a big red planet."

"Remmie, how come you always remind me about my name?"

The pair made it past an old live oak tree dwarfing overhead. Once behind the cover of the tree's enormous trunk, Remmie stood and put her hand on Jupiter's shoulder. "Jupiter," she searched for words on the tops of her black leather boots, but then looked him at him as if she were a sage delivering wisdom to an apprentice. "Anyone named after a planet has...has great things in their future." For all her youth, spunk, and energy, Remmie carried inside her the wise soul of an eighty-year-old woman.

The boy looked back at her with words scrambling across his mind, but said nothing.

The pair skipped up the path across a bald patch of sandhill and made for the trail that led further into the heavy trees. As the upper canopy of the forest rose above them, beams of sunlight shimmered across the tops of their heads, illuminating them in fits and starts, like gentle fingers. They were free and clear of the sight of any adult and laughed as they slowed their pace.

The canopy of trees was comprised of live oak, hickory, pine, and a smattering of chestnut oaks whose enormous acorns were favored by whitetail deer and wild hogs alike. The hardwood trees were adorned in Spanish moss—nature's tinsel—which clung to branches and dangled almost to the ground in some spots. Well below the pillaring trees that stretched towards the sky, the understory of the forest was covered in broad, leafy palmetto plants that grew in clumps and bunches, stretching out in all directions.

Mr. Winkles slowed the children and knelt down amongst them. "Now y'all take a look around this forest." I want you to notice something. See how tall the trees are? Now, look down around here, down where we're standing. See that? There's all this low stuff growing on the ground. Anybody see anything that's missing?" They all looked around, wishing to be the first to answer the question. The answer eluded them until, at last, Lenny lifted a timid hand into the air.

"Mr. Winkles, it seems to me there are a bunch of tall trees way up there, and a bunch a short plalnts way down here, but, there aren't any trees or plants or anything in the middle."

"You've got the instincts of a rattle snake that knows when it's time to skitter away, you know that? He's exactly right, yessirree, sure as you're born, he is. See, this is exactly how the slave drivers see themselves. They see themselves as the tall trees towering over the slaves below. But you know something? They're wrong, yessirree. Y'all listen to old Mr. Winkles," he lowered his voice again to a whisper. The kids began to recognize it as a signal he was about to say something important. "No man can ever can reign above another man. It's not in God's way of being, that is. See, God didn't put man on earth so he can reign above other men, especially after he sent his only son to come down here for each and every one of us." He stood tall, "And these trees are full grown, aren't they? But there isn't any fault in them. They're just doing what God intended them to do, and they don't mean any harm. I sure wish the drivers understood that, sure as you're born, I do."

5
No Moss on this Path

"Hey," said Remmie, "how come we've never gone down this path?"

"Every day, every day," said Jupiter, shaking his head. "You funny, you know that? You're about as funny as one of them biting bugs, a no-see-um, wanting to grow up to be a mosquito. Remmie, you *know* why we've never been down that path. We both know why." The pair stared down the narrow wooded path, just barely trampled enough to hold back moss from growing on it. It twisted off to the left, and led into a dark, low place, thick with vegetation. Beyond the entrance to the path was the unknown, a place the drivers had warned them repeatedly never to set foot on. They said it was dangerous, and that it was guarded by the spirit of an old witch. Legend had it, they said, that in the 1600's the woman had been suspected by the townspeople of being a witch. She was cast out of society, and late one moonless and stormy night, men on horseback came for her. She was burned at the stake for what they called *heresy*, the belief in something that goes against the teachings of the church. In truth, she was innocent. Just as they lit the fire, she yelled out to them in blood-curdling anger, swearing they would never know peace again. And supposedly, this was the very spot it happened. The drivers said late at night, she would often be seen patrolling the nearby woods, a spectral dark blur in search of her killers, long since passed.

"Oh, come on," jibed Remmie. "There isn't anything to that old tale the drivers are always telling us. There's no witch down there. They're just trying to scare us."

But before she could even lean her body weight forward to step in the direction of the path, Jupiter jumped in front of her. "No Remmie, no," he said. "I'm scared. That witch is down there. We can't go down that path. Just look at that path. It ain't right. There is just something about that place." He looked down the path as a soft shiver jittered up his spine. The two got quiet, and Jupiter spoke in a hushed voice, "Ever notice how there isn't any moss hanging on the trees down this path? You just look around. There's Spanish moss on all the trees around here. All of them! But ain't no moss hanging from them trees down there. It ain't right, I'm tellin' ya. It ain't right."

Remmie gave him a look and started to push past. But Remmie had a heart for her friend and a loyalty that was as unmeasured as the number of grains of sand on the beach. "Okay. Okay Jupiter. We won't go down there, not yet anyway. But I still say there's no witch. I don't know what's down there, but we have to find out. Soon we have to go down there, Jupiter." The two children skipped off in the other direction, away from the thicket.

In the quiet of the forest on this windless day, their childlike voices could be heard, faintly echoing in the distance. It was the sound of laughter. Mr. Winkles and the children walked a short distance down the forbidden path until it gave up its secret—a large, rusty pot with copper tube spiraling out of it, and the remains of charred embers from a recent campfire underneath.

The children did not know what the object was, and the old man did not immediately address the topic. Instead, he spoke quietly, "Some say that each of our emotions has a color all its own." Then, as wonderful sounds of laughter echoed off the trunks of neighboring live oak trees, the feint color of green with swirls of yellow began to glow from a place further down the trail.

Lenny stared into the colors, tugged on the old man's sleeve, and spoke before bothering to wait for permission. "I'm scared. I'm afraid of that witch."

"Oh, goodness, now," said Mr. Winkles. "Don't you be scared Meestah Lenny. Don't you be scared none. There is no witch, and even if there was, old Mr. Winkles is right here and I'm going protect you. All y'all gather around and listen. Ain't nothing be afraid of, yessirree, nothing at all. Hey!" said Winkles in sudden excitement, "can y'all keep a secret?"

The children again looked at one other, then at Lenny. Lenny nodded his ascent to Mr. Winkles. "Now, I know that Remmie and Jupiter think there's something spooky about this trail we're on, but, you know what? Like I said, there's no witch down here. Nossirree, there's no witch down here at all." Then his eyebrows cocked upwards and he said, "But I'm here to tell you what is down this path. It's a still."

The children stared, some tilting their head to the side. Lenny, who had become the de facto spokesperson for the group, cleared his throat, then said, "What's a still, Mr. Winkles?"

"A still? Oh!" laughed the man, "A still is what they use to make moonshine whiskey. Y'all know what moonshine is?" The children nodded in ascent. "Yessirree, they make moonshine from a big old contraption called a still. And, if the truth be told, nobody is supposed to make moonshine."

"And that's why the driver men told Remmie and Jupiter to stay away from the path? Because they have a still down here?"

"You're right as rain, Lenny."

The children seemed satisfied with the explanation.

"But Mr. Winkles, what did you mean a minute ago when you said, *our motions have a color*?"

"Oh, well, that's e-motions, my good Lenny, e-motions. Well see, out here in Gods good nature, each person's emotions put off a kind of energy. Kind of like when you toss a big rock into a pond. Well, that rock makes a splash, doesn't it? And the splash makes ripples in the water that spread out in all directions. It's like that. Each time a person has emotions, if you look real hard, you can see those emotions in color all around you. If they're mad, you might see red, or if they're happy, you might see the greenest green, or yellowest yellow, or sometimes orange. Does that make sense?"

"Is this part of the wonderment, joy, merriment, and magic you keep talking about?"

"Yes, Meestah Lenny, yes it is."

6
The Pointing of the Cypress

It wasn't much longer, perhaps only a few hours later, when Remmie's curiosity got the best of her. She headed straight towards the forbidden trail. When they arrived at the entrance Remmie perched her eyebrows at Jupiter. He knew this meant trouble. "Bok, bok, bok," she chirped. "Bokbokbokbok, Jupiter's a chiiiicken, Jupiter's a chiiiicken," the singing continued.

"Oh, you just hush," recanted Jupiter. "I ain't no chicken."

"Well then," said Remmie, "if you *ain't* no chicken, then prove it. Follow me. Jupiter, there is no witch. I'm telling you, there is no witch. Now come on." She skipped down the path into the dark thicket leading to the still with a grin on her face too powerful to conceal as much as she tried.

Jupiter looked back over his shoulder, scanning the tops of the palmettos, and listening closely the way one might when hunting deer, or turkey. Satisfied that no one was around, he ducked down just below the height of the palmettos and rambled forward after Remmie, trying to catch up. He had fear in his heart and a sense that they weren't alone. "Remmie! Wait up," he whispered, though it was unlikely she could hear over the crunching of live oak leaves underneath her feet. "Remmieeeeee," he repeated. Jupiter caught up to her after the path rounded to the right, and then curved to the left.

Remmie stood straight and erect, then placed her hands on her hips and began nodding her head up and down. "See this here?" In front of her was the huge tin pot with spiraling copper tubing, sealed from end to end. It was covered with a fresh layer of palmetto fronds, each one about two feet across. The leaves formed huge star-like shapes, and were intertwined with one other, like pairs of hands readying to pray. The palmetto fronds made a feeble attempt to camouflage the still from prying eyes. "This is why the drivers are always telling us to stay out of here. There are no witches or ghosts down here. They're just trying to keep us from finding out that they're making moonshine. My papa would not approve of this."

"But what is it?" said Jupiter.

"Well you big dummy," replied Remmie, "it's a still. You've never heard of a still?"

"I ain't no dummy."

Remmie thought back about her words, and then said in a soft voice, "I know, I know. You aren't a dummy. I shouldn't have said it, Jupiter. I'm sorry." Their friendship stretched back as far as either could remember. At first, Remmie's parents thought the friendship harmless, but now that his daughter was getting older, Remmie's father began to think it unwise to allow her to associate with a slave that she'd own one day. The two children lived only a few hundred yards from one another, yet were from different worlds, one black, one white. The distance between their houses may as well have been the width of the ocean that separated Georgia's Golden Isles from the West coast of Africa.

Looking down, Jupiter said, "That's okay Remmie," as his feet shifted live-oak leaves side to side.

The path terminated at the still, yet Remmie, who had never been bold enough to explore this forbidden corner of the swampy forest, wanted to see more. She used both hands to separate a thick shock of palmettos and turned her body sideways, and bulled her way through.

"Remmie, where you going?" said Jupiter, almost afraid not to follow her. He got down on his hands and knees and crawled through the less dense undergrowth until his head stuck out the other side like a turtle. "Oh, lookey there. It's so beautiful, but what happened to them cypress trees?"

He crawled forward and stood next to Remmie, her mouth agape at what lay before her. They had stumbled upon a lowland, brilliantly lit with coursing sunbeams—the darkness of the forest just behind them, gone. Ahead of them, standing in a broad opening like sentinels in the stark light, were a small group of withered, gray cypress trees, each only about ten feet tall. The long-since-dead trees were the color of sun bleached ash, and stood twisted and gnarled against the ravages of nature and time. The trees were lined in two rows that together formed into the shape similar to an arrowhead—five trees on each side leading up to a single tree to form the tip of the arrow. One tree, the only one to have toppled, laid out of place at the back of the arrow, crumpled in a heap of rotting pulp, its ash gray color having given way to putrid black.

"Isn't that strange," questioned Remmie.

"What?"

"This one tree. It's all rotted."

Jupiter replied, "What's so strange about that? It's just a dead tree that fell over and is rotting."

"No, Jupiter, these are *cypress* trees. Even after they die, they don't just rot, the wood stays and stays and stays. And besides, look at all of them. They're about the same size. They've been dead a long time, yet this one fell over and is rotted. I mean, look around here. Even the branches that fell off the other trees aren't rotted like this one."

The unlikely pair stared across the opening in the marsh, scanning for anything else unusual. Remmie broke the silence, "It's like they're pointing," she said. "Like they're pointing the way. They're pointing over that way, deeper into the woods on the other side."

"What do you mean they're pointing?...oh, I see it. Yeah, it's like these cypress trees are standing there in a perfect arrow. Well, all except this rotted one here."

Remmie walked forward past the closest tree, splayed out on its side, "Yeah, kind of strange, isn't it? The other trees are all lined up, perfect-like. Almost as if they were planted. But this one in the back, it's not just that it fell over and rotted, it's out of place. It's like, somehow, it doesn't belong." She looked Jupiter in the eye, "You know we've got to keep going and find what they're a pointing at, don't you?"

Jupiter crossed his arms, "I just knew you were going to say that."

7
Rotten

Mr. Winkles walked the children past the still, then pushed against the thick palmettos, and forced them to yield a thin opening. As the children came out of the darkness and into the bright light of the area Remmie and Jupiter had just left, muffled ooo's and aaah's abound. Coming into the small circular marsh, with all its brilliant light and spectacular dwarf cypress trees, was like stumbling into a fairytale where all was right with the world.

Before Lenny could even begin tugging against Mr. Winkles' sweater, the old man looked down in anticipation, smiling.

"Um, um, um, Mr. Winkles? Why'd all those little trees die? They're so pretty."

Mr. Winkles put his hand on the back of Lenny's head, "The mind of a child is a wonderful thing. Yessirree, it is. Well, that's what I brought y'all here to see."

"The trees?"

"That's right, the trees," he said, his hand wove across the span in front of them. "Y'all all step down onto this marsh, and take a look to these trees. Its okay, the ground ain't muddy because the tide is out. And besides, it's only a really high tide that comes all the way up into here. So, most days, it's not muddy up in here at all."

Children stepped off the edge of the isle and down onto the hard marsh. Their feet felt the change from pine needles to marsh grass and dark earth. "Y'all all get up close to these cypress trees; get real close to them. Go ahead, get on up there, that's it. Now, y'all put your hands onto the trunk and branches of one of the little trees. Feel how it feels on your hands." Each child placed a hand, and sometimes two, on the surface of the cypress in front of them. There was one child per tree, except that nearest Mr. Winkles, Lenny shared the space with another. None of the children stood beside the rotted tree.

"It's so smooth," said Lenny, "but, it's so wavy." Lenny's hand moved back and forth on the tree trunk which spanned only about eight inches in diameter. The surface was knurled with twists and swirls etched into the wood. The rays of sunlight cracked through the cloud cover, and put a shine onto the little enclave.

Some of the surface texture of the wood looked like the forward rushing of a river, whereas other areas nearest to where a branch protruded from the trunk, formed concentric circular patterns emanating further and further from the branch. In one place, Lenny saw a tiny branch sticking off, yet it was broken, only about three inches from the twisted trunk. The swirling shapes of the wood surrounding the tiny aperture made it look like the handle of a knife, the blade buried underneath. At the lowest part of the trunk, three swirls in the wood pooled together and formed what looked like a face, the eyes and nose twisted out of proportion. The grain of the wood was etched deeper here, as though the burden of supporting the weight of the trunk had taken its toll after centuries of weather.

"That's it," said Winkles, "that's good. Y'all feel the surface of the trees. They've been sitting there for hundreds of years. Hadn't changed much. Feel across the lichens and moss. They're part of this here earth too." He smiled, "Y'all haven't ever gotten down close to mother nature, have you? No, y'all spent too much time cooped up in that classroom of yours, or playing your iPads and stuff." He then gestured up to the sky, "You've got to get out and get up close to nature. It's not something you can learn from a book, it's something you have to touch, to feel, to smell." The kids all inhaled, imitating Mr. Winkles. "And kneel down here to the marsh dirt. Get your head down close to it. Y'all smell it? It's clean, isn't it? All the dirt and such that you all are used to smelling doesn't smell good, does it? But the dirt down here in the marsh is all cleaned out. That's part of what the marsh is supposed to do.

"And look over there to that saltwater creek. Know what lives in there? They're blue crabs, oy-stahs, shrimp, and, anybody guess what else?"

Lenny's hand jarred upwards, "Alligators." Some of the others looked at him in a moment of rigidness, and then stood, readying to run.

"That's right, Meestah Lenny. You're as smart as anything, you know that? Alligators. But, don't y'all worry none, they don't just come up and say hello. They're kind of scared of us too, yessirree. Alright, now, y'all put a hand on this grass. Its tall grass, isn't it? All the way up to your waist. We call this *cord* grass. Yessirree. And y'all look down in between the cord grass, down there in the dirt. What else do you see?"

"Well, there's some shell looking things. Funny though, they're halfway buried in there," said Lenny.

"Those are clams, Lenny. Not exactly the kind of clams you eat, but I suppose you could if you were hungry enough. Go ahead, I know y'all want to. Go ahead and pull one up. Don't hurt it none though. Remember, that's a live little clam inside there. Yessirree, y'all take a good look at its shell, and then when you're done, put them back right where you found them, nice and gentle-like."

"Wow," said Lenny, "I never really just looked at stuff like this before. There's a whole little world down inside each little place, if you look hard enough."

"Yessirree," said Mr. Winkles, "yessirree."

"Is that why you wanted us to look close?"

"Well, sort of," laughed Winkles. "But I had something else in mind too. So, now that you've all looked at things real close, did you look at this little place from afar as well? You can't just look at things up close. You've got to look from afar too. Did y'all notice anything? Uh, maybe y'all should step back here, and look from this side." Each child walked back towards the old grandfather and stood near the rotting tree. Each stared, straining to find out what it was they were to notice, each wishing they could be the one to discover it first.

After several moments, Lenny said, "Well, all these cypress trees. It's like, it's like they're so perfectly planted, in rows. Those ones in the front of this dead one are all pointing. Pointing over in that direction over there."

"You're right as rain, Lenny, right as rain, yessirree. These trees are pointing right over yonder," he said, holding out a crinkled hand. "Uh, let me ask you all this. How many trees are there?"

"...Nine, ten, eleven. There's eleven trees."

"You sure about that counting Lenny?"

"Oh, well, if you're counting this dead one, then there are twelve."

Winkles perked his chin up, "And how many of you are there?"

"There are twelve of us!" blurted out a little girl.

"Yes ma'am. Twelve of you and twelve cypresses. Twelve twisted, swirly cypress trees. Now y'all all gather around. I'm gonna tell you something about these trees." Mr. Winkles knelt down on one knee as the children circled around him. He looked like a football coach with arthritis preparing to give his team the big speech. "Twelve, hmmm, twelve. Twelve, twelve, twelve." He peered across each set of squinting eyes. "There are twelve of you, and twelve trees. Y'all remember your Sunday school classes? The bible talked about twelve disciples too, didn't it?" He surveyed their surprised responses. "You see, every one of us," he pointed down at Lenny, smiling, "that means you too, Lenny. Every one of us is supposed to carry the message forth, the message about God and Jesus. We're supposed to talk to folks about God and Jesus and all that." He knelt an elbow on his knee then pointed at the trees, "Jesus had twelve disciples, didn't he? The twelve disciples did just that, they carried the message out to all the folks. Sometimes when God gives us a job, we describe that as a *calling*. They were called, you might say, called to help spread the word of God." He lowered his voice, "And you are too. That's right, just as sure as you're born. Y'all all are called to carry it forward too, just like the twelve disciples. These twelve trees represent the twelve disciples, and they represent you too."

The little girl turned around, staring at the trees, then said, "But Mr. Winkles, what about this tree? This rotten one. What happened to it? If the twelve disciples were supposed to carry the story of Jesus to all the folks, didn't this tree carry out the word of God or anything?"

"Oooo, you're a smart one too!" said Winkles. "I declare. You see, not every person that is called, answers that call. See, some folks are too busy; they're too busy doing their job, or getting all distracted about things they think are important, and they don't answer the call, or they're not even listening in the first place. That's why I had you all look real close at these cypress trees so y'all would see how important it is to slow down, get quiet, and notice things. You can't hear God calling you if you don't get quiet. Lenny, who is that rotten tree supposed to be?"

Lenny closed his eyes until they strained, but opened them into confused blankness.

"If these trees are the twelve disciples, this rotten tree is Judas." The children nodded their understanding. "Judas was one of the twelve disciples, and in the end, he betrayed Jesus. Now, some folks say Judas was a bad, bad man. Others though, say he was just fulfilling the prophecy that Jesus was to be betrayed anyway, and without Judas carrying out that prophecy, Jesus never would have been sacrificed, which was the whole point to begin with."

"Wait," said Lenny. "What? What do you mean it was the whole point to begin with?"

"Lenny, God the Father had a plan. See, all the time, folks were sinning against God and against each other, just like they do today too. But sin isn't free. Sin has a cost to it. And that cost has to be paid. God's plan was to give up his only son as a sacrifice to pay the cost of all those sins. So, Judas was a part of God's plan. Judas had a job, and that job was to betray Jesus so that he would be caught and put to death. Jesus' death is the price that had to be paid for all of our sins." He paused, then rose and said, "Come on, we got a lot more to see."

8

A Baby Hurricane

On the west coast of Africa, in the country of Gabon, an explorer named Paul du Chaillu, an American of French and African descent, looked across a sliver of beach at the mouth of the Komo river and squinted against the brilliant glare of sunlight. Just across the river lay a settlement of then famous African men. Only two years prior, the French navy had intercepted an illegal slave ship near the mouth of the Komo, seized it, and set the captives free on the spot. As du Chaillu prepared to embark on an exploration deep into the interior of the Dark Continent, he could only wonder what the scene two years ago must have been like. Since the men had been abducted from all parts of the African interior, none really knew how to journey back to their homelands. So, they established a hamlet and named it *Baraka*, which, in the local Shira language, meant 'free town'. Some in the hamlet would later confirm being freed from a slave ship by the French. Others, however, would speak of Freetown as having been formed when the ancestors of the Gullah people walked across the ocean from America and back to the African coast.

As du Chaillu turned around to gaze onto the endless waters of the Gulf of Guinea, he stared into the ominous darkness of a thunderhead, far out in the bay. He noted to a zoologist colleague in a muddle of English and French, "We are most fortunate, for the storm brewing here in our midst is enormous, but is headed out to sea."

In those days, no one knew that nature's largest hurricanes often formed off the African coast, before swirling their way towards the Americas.

9
Grief Thick and Wet

The plantation house had stood on this spot since just after the Revolutionary War and had been served by house slaves since its construction. The starched white columns were the first thing to catch the eye, which was the architect's intent. The wrap-around porch spanned fourteen feet in width all the way around and served to greet guests, albeit in an ostentatious manner. Sixteen rooms in all, including one about the size of a good cupboard, for Fanny, who had served as a slave inside the stately manor for the past thirty years.

Fanny ambled forth from her room each morning to bring the house to order. And, if the truth be told, most nights she was awakened at least once to fetch water or tonic or some other such unnecessary for "Mastah Grayd'n," the owner of the plantation—Remmie's father. Graydon Moon earned his money the really old fashioned way, he inherited it. His father first made his fortune in the dry goods business, but later expanded into cotton and rice. The Moon Plantation was once one of the largest exporters of rice in the state of Georgia, and Graydon aimed to return it to those glory days. Graydon, however, was not as astute in the ways of business as his father whose Harvard education made him one of the elite. His father enshrouded himself inside the inner workings of "the aristocracy of the South," as it was known—an exclusive group of the wealthiest men.

Graydon lost his wife to an accident two years prior. And although he would never say as much, he blamed Remmie for it. In truth, the child had nothing to do with it. She had simply broken her handheld chalkboard that was used daily in her school work. Mrs. Moon was on her way to town to fetch a new one when the accident happened. Graydon was never the same after that. It was as if his whole world collapsed around him. Thick, wet grief formed a drapery that seemed to hang over his head, across his shoulders, and down to his feet. The weight of it pushed down on him to a point where he almost walked in a humped-over manner. It wasn't an exhausting thing to carry, but more something akin to wearing a heavy pair of over-sized boots—one only notices how heavy they are once they are taken off.

He lived in darkness with his grief, and darkness can be a powerful thing. Darkness has a pull to it, not the pull of a magnet, but more like the way a person feels compelled to stare at a full moon, at the ocean waves, or a campfire as flames of liquid light shimmer and dance. Averting one's glance takes effort. Darkness is seductive like that, and that type of seduction creates a call, and that call is insatiable.

The children shuffled behind Mr. Winkles as he made his way from the woods, all the way back to the plantation house. He led them behind the house then came up its side, staying just out of sight. Lenny was staring so intently in the direction of the front doors as the group moved up the side of the house, that he didn't notice Winkles stop. The boy bumped into the back of the old man. "Oh, excuse me," he said, pushing his thick black glasses higher on his nose.

"You're fine Meestah Lenny, you be just fine." Mr. Winkles ruffled the boy's hair. "Everybody stay quiet now, y'all just squat down low here next to these bushes."

"What are we doing?" asked Lenny.

"I want to show you Remmie's papa. He'll be along any minute now, I expect. Oooo, there he is! Hush now, hush. Get down."

Graydon Moon walked out the huge double doors with purpose, wearing the clothes of a scholar, an attorney, or perhaps a member of the local magistrate. Out on the porch, he stood at the top of the steps and yelled, "Mordecai! Mordecai!" calling after the head slave driver.

Down on the river bank, the slave driver looked over his shoulder towards the grand house and then spat a wallop of chewing tobacco onto the sand. "Oh what's eatin' at his drawers already?" he said. He started a brisk walk towards the house and called back, "Yassir, be there accordingly." The man stunk of three days sweat, and wore a general disregard for his countenance the way other men might wear a new suit; his repulsiveness was something he almost prided himself in.

As Mordecai walked underneath the sprawling magnolia trees, he tripped on a tall tree root poking just above the surface, flopped face down, and skidded across the pool of slick magnolia leaves. He started to curse, but caught himself before the foul words eased out.

"That man's got a mean temper, yessirree," whispered Mr. Winkles. "Any man that takes pleasure in the mistreatment of another man is somebody who's got his faith wrong."

"My Lord, Mordecai," said Graydon Moon, holding a starched white handkerchief to his mouth. "Watch your step, man, watch your step."

Mordecai brushed the dry leaf chips from his torso, "Yassir, yassir." Then just underneath his breath he parroted back, "Watch your step Mordecai." It sounded like a seven-year-old schoolgirl imitating her teacher.

"Now," continued Graydon from atop the steps, "like we discussed yesterday, I don't want those men treated so harshly. I hire you to do my bidding, and what I say goes." Graydon looked down at the man with his head cocked sideways, judging the coming response before it was uttered.

The slave driver's shoulders remained slumped, "Sir, we've been over this before. I run my slaves the way I run my slaves." He was throwing down a gauntlet, testing Graydon's resolve. "I been doin' this since before you was borned, and I'm knowin' how to get men to do what needs to be done."

Graydon's head tilted up so his view of Mordecai was obscured by his own nose. "Your slaves? *Your* slaves? May I remind you who pays the mortgage on the property around here? Who pays the debenture due to feed suppliers in town, who pays the..." It was clear Graydon Moon was upset, but clearer still was his unwillingness to force the issue over harsh treatment of the slaves.

"Yassir, I know you pay my salary, Mr. Grayd'n, but I know what I'm doing and I ain't about to change it." With that, he spat on the ground once more.

"Very well, but if I find one of the men hurt unnecessarily...there will...there'll be a price to pay for the one responsible, understood?"

"Yassir," said Mordecai, whose face tilted in a manner consistent of one leaning his head against the stock of a rifle. The slight grin widened—he knew he had won.

"Now," continued the pretentious Graydon Moon as he tamped a handkerchief to his forehead, "what is your progress on the new rice field this morning?"

"Well, sir, yesterdee we done finished pullin' the stumps outta plot number four. Well, we almost finished. We just got one more stump to pull, so we ought to be able to set the gate posts by this here afternoon."

Graydon slapped the handkerchief into his open hand repeatedly, as if it were a riding crop, "So, you're telling me my new rice plot will be operational for planting by tomorrow morning. Am I correct?"

"Yassir, she'll be ready. We'll get the gate up, an we'll be plantin' rice seed at the same time. Once them seeds is in the ground, we'll open the gate and let her flood."

"Very well," said Graydon. He leaned in close as if to deliver an ultimatum, "I expect planting to be done by tomorrow, and by the following morning, I better see six feet of water covering that plot."

Mordecai waited before answering. It was his little rebellion. "Yassir."

10
Of Rice and Tides

Lenny tugged on the back of the sweater, "Mr. Winkles? Mr. Winkles, Mr. Winkles..."

"Yes, Lenny, yes. Just calm down there, big fella." Winkles spun around to face the child. He put his hand on the boy's cheek. "Now, what can I do for you?"

"Um, um, I don't understand," said Lenny, staring off at the rice plot, "how do they do it? What's that talk about a gate and flooding the field? What's, what's, what's..."

Winkles leaned back laughing, and caught himself before tipping backwards. "Lenny, my little man, so full'a questions. Well, alright, y'all all circle up now, you hear? You all in the back, come on up and gather around. Okay, so way back here in the windey, warm, waterway, way deeeep down south, the plantation owners grow lots and lots of rice. You see that there rice plot over yonder? Well, what they do is, the men first build up what they call a *dike* all the way round the place where they want to grow the rice. That helps hold in all the water that the rice needs for growin'."

"But, but," stuttered Lenny, "with a dike built all around there, how do they get the water in? How do they get it out?"

"My, my, my. I said it once, and I'll say it again. You're a smart one Meestah Lenny, a smart one, yessirree! See, some of this water around here flows in from the river and moves its way out to sea. But since we're so close to the ocean, the tide pushes its way back up these rivers too. Just as sure as you're born, it does. Twice a day, the tide comes way, way up high, and it pushes all that ocean water up this river and up these finger creeks. The tides around here moves up and down around six, sometimes even eight feet high!"

Lenny was awestruck, "Eight feet of water? So, the water in that empty looking creek down there is going to go up eight feet, today?"

"Yessirree!" said Winkles, "Happens twice a day, it does. The way they build a rice field is they get the dike built all the way around into the shape of a big square. That makes up a rice field. Then they wait until its *low* tide. Then, they cut a wide hole in one part of the dirt wall of the dike, and all the water inside of the rice field just flows out with the tide. After it flows out, they put up some posts and a wooden gate where that hole was. They close the gate by sticking two other big posts into the mud; one on the inside of the gate, and one on the outside, blocking the gate so it can't open any more and the tide can't get back in."

"Wow, that's amazing," said Lenny.

Winkles continued, "Then, they cut down all the trees inside that new rice plot, and haul them out. The trees are sold for lumber, yessirree. Then, once the plot is ready, they plant the rice seeds. And Lenny, you're gonna love this part. Rice loves to grow in a whole bunch'a water. So, after they're done planting the rice seeds, they remove the post on the inside of the gate. The next time high tide comes, the water goes floodin' in there because the gate can swing open."

"But, but, Mr. Winkles," clamored Lenny, "won't the water just wash on out when it gets to be low tide again?"

"Oh, no. Since the post on the outside of the gate is still there, the water inside the dike pushes against it as soon as the tide goes out, and it closes tight, trapping that water inside." The children's eyes went wide. "Months later, when the rice is fully grown, they let that gate open again, and the water flows out so they can go in there an harvest the rice." Children looked back and forth at one another with wide smiles.

"Well? What's the next part?" said Lenny.

"The next part, huh." It was more of a statement than a question.

"Yeah, Mr. Winkles, after you teach us about something, there's always a next part that you want us to know about."

"Yessirree, you sure are right, right as rain." The group leaned towards one another as the man's expression sombered. "See, that rice field? It's no ordinary rice field. I wanted y'all to see it because in our story today it has a special meaning. That rice field represents something, something important. That rice field represents your soul."

"It does?" said the little girl as her brunette pigtails bounced.

"Sure does, Missy. See, your soul starts out kind of barren. It's got nothing it knows to go do. But then, God plants seeds in your soul, and those seeds grow into *purpose*. It's God that gives us our purpose."

"You mean there are rice seeds growing inside me?" said Lenny.

Winkles smiled, "Well, not exactly rice seeds, but instead, they're the seeds God puts into your heart. They're the things he wants for you, or wants you to do. And lots of them are the *people* he's brought into your life. People that maybe need your help, or even people that are planted there to help you, like your friends. And the seeds grow into things. They grow into all kinds of things. Things for you to do, things your supposed to feel. They represent *purpose*, and usually those things are *Gods'* purpose, just for you and only you." He paused to see the flicker in the eyes of each child. It is something that is lost lest one takes notice quickly. "Yessirree," he said, "God is planting seeds in us all the time. Then, to make these seeds grow, he brings his love into our hearts."

"I know!" said Lenny, his hand shot high into the air. "The water that floods into the rice field is the love! Is that the love?" Lenny's grin exploded into pride.

"Yessirree, you bet it is. The high tide waters are God's love that he gives to all of us. That water's kind of like the holy spirit that flows into all of us. Without that water, the rice seeds out there wouldn't grow none at all. And without God's love, there wouldn't be anything to make our souls into such beautiful places, places that grow great things," his hand pointed at each child in turn.

The kids began whispering to one another, a few pointing at the far right side of the dike surrounding the enclosed the field. "Now, what are y'all talking about back there?" laughed Winkles.

A little girl in the back lowered her head. "I just..." she stopped and looked down.

"Now that's okay, little miss. You can tell old Mr. Winkles. What are you wondering about?"

She looked up and peered through fine hair, the color of a chestnut oak leaf in fall. "I was wondering about the wooden gate."

"Well now, what about that gate?" Mr. Winkles had a way of disarming a person's shyness to a point where it gave up, and ran forward waving a little white flag.

"Well, if the rice field is our soul, and the rice seeds are all the stuff God puts in there to give us purpose, and the water is the love, then what's the gate?"

Winkles rubbed his grizzled chin, "The gate. Hmmm, well, you know, that's a good-un, a gooood-un, yessirree." This time there was something different in his demeanor. Perhaps it was the way his head cocked upwards, or the seriousness of his eyes that told the children he was about to tell them something they knew they should hear. "Children, I want to tell y'all something, and I want you all to understand it, because it's important, real important. See that gate out yonder? Well, notice that that gate swings both inward, towards the rice field, and outward, towards the river. The swinging of that gate happens in one direction or the other depending on which side of the gate the men put up a post on it." Winkles scanned their eyes. He could see they were listening, but not yet tracking. "That gate is kind of important, isn't it? Yessirree. That gate has a kind of control on the rice, doesn't it? I mean, if the men put a post on one side, the tide water comes in, and stays in, right? Or, it they put it on the other side, the water can't get in there, can it? So, if the water, or the *love of God*, isn't in the rice field, ain't no rice gonna grow, is it?" Most children shook their heads, and then turned to look back at the gate. He then said what he'd come to say, "That gate represents what we call *choice*."

"Choice? I, I, I don't understand. Choice for what?" said Lenny.

Winkles leaned in close to the boy, "Choice of whether or not we will accept God's love or not. See, God's love is always there, isn't it? Just like that tide water is always there. The tide is gonna come in every day, twice a day, no matter what we do. And God's love is gonna try to get into your heart every day no matter what you do too. There's no stopping it from trying, nossirree. But, and here's the important part, if you don't let it in, because you've got your gate closed, it can't go to work helping the seeds he planted on your soul to grow. You'd just be wandering around this whole world with no direction in your life. And y'all all think about this. You ever see what happens to a seed if you just plant it, and don't show it any love? Don't give it enough water and such? It grows real slow. Sometimes it doesn't grow at all, and just withers away. Other times...it grows crooked."

Lenny's lower lip began a slow, but steady quiver, and his eyes moistened, "But, but, but how do I know my gate is open?"

"Meestah Lenny, now you just look into the twinkle-winkle of my eye. Look down in there deep now. Every time you take notice of something beautiful, every time you smile, every time you do something nice for somebody you've never met before, every time you gaze at a rainbow, or see a sunset, you feel something warm inside, don't you? Well, that warm feeling, that's the love of God pouring in on your heart. Yessirree, it's just as warm as this tidewater on a summer day. But you have to *choose* it. You've got to choose to let God in your heart. And do you know what? The more you let in God's love, the more he's in there, and the more the seeds grow. And the more them seeds grow, the more beauty you're going to see, and the more love there is, and the more you going to want to share it."

11
Engineering the Rice Field

Even though it was early, the men toiled in what was starting to become a scorching hot day. Humidity levels were always high on the Georgia coast, and combined with a cloudless sky, conditions could become downright brutal. Yet, it wasn't the presence of high heat that was the worst of it. No, that was reserved for three of the coast's favorite insects. First, the mosquitoes, whose ability to proliferate and inhabit every square inch of air space was uncanny. And second, what coastal Georgians called "no-seeums." No-seeums are a tiny version of biting fly that is barely noticed, both by eye and to the touch. But, after they lay their sucking mouth parts into the flesh, the resulting whelp makes that of a mosquito pale in comparison. Coming in a close third are the larger biting horseflies. Heinous in their creation, their only purpose seems to be to torment all to whom they come in contact.

On this particular morning, the slave men were fighting in a last-ditch attempt to clear the final stump from the rice field before planting could begin. Clearing the trees themselves was a herculean effort in and of itself, yet removing the stumps they left behind proved to be the most difficult part of the job. It was back-breaking work, not to mention the horrendous presence of the slave drivers; never satisfied, never at ease, and as far as the slaves could tell, never right with God—an abomination.

The mud on the virgin rice field was as thick as molasses mixed with sap from a pine tree. Three men stood knee deep in the dark sludge which had been built over eons of rotting plants, leaves, wood pulp, and silt. The stump was leaning in one direction, fighting against every pull to the contrary. Ropes lassoed over the top of the stump led off about thirty feet to the dike, where a dozen slaves gripped one of two lines, and pulled in unison. Jupiter's father, Washington, was the only man pushing against the stump, instead of pulling the ropes. Washington held a few special privileges. He had the mind of an engineer, and the heart of a shepherd. He had a talent for seeing the engineering possibilities and constraints in a way unlike any white man in the county. That talent often put him in charge of the most difficult projects. In fact, there were times in which Mordecai would consult with Washington before starting a difficult project, although, he would never admit to that.

"Leander! Leander," yelled the driver to a seventeen-year-old slave, "drop that rope and get down there with that hatchet! When they pull the stump, and it leans forward, jump down under there and cut at them roots, boy."

"Yassuh. But suh? If'n they can't hold it, an' I'm under it, it might fall back on me," squeaked the seventeen-year-old.

"You'll shut yer mouth and do what yer told, if you know what's good for you. You're the only one small enough to fit." Mordecai, wiped his forehead against the filthy sleeve of his shirt which didn't look like it had ever been washed. The pressure to clear the rice field and get it ready for planting weighed on his shoulders. "Alright now, this here time, y'all all gonna pull at the same time, and hold it tight. Once the stump is leanin' this way, Leander's gonna get down under it and go to choppin' at the roots. And, if you don't want him crushed, well, I be guessin' you gonna hold them lines tight, ain't ya?" A sinister grin pursed across his face, revealing itself from underneath five days of stubble. Mordecai's teeth were the color of brown pearls soaked in kerosene. But, in reality, he was nervous as well. If a slave was badly injured or even killed under his watch, there would be a high price to pay. The financial value of a slave, particularly one of young age, was immense.

Washington looked down at the depth of the hole the stump created, and thought about this boy, Leander. A seventeen-year-old—if something happened, how could he explain it to his mother? The mother had already suffered so much when her husband, Leander's father, was sold to a slave plantation in

Louisiana, and taken away. Neither Leander, nor his mother, could tolerate any further loss.

Washington walked behind the stump and studied it. He knew how hard it was to keep upright as the men pulled against it with the ropes. The smell of mud oozing from underneath the stump was a cross between rotting leaves and spoiled eggs. Although Washington was accustomed to it, it turned his head. The risk was immense, and fear rose inside him the way mercury raises in a thermometer—but neither had any choice. To disobey meant the whip.

"Alright! Y'all get ready," yelled Mordecai to the slaves. "Leander, don't you wait none, boy. Soon as they get the stump up a bit, I don't want to see you still standing up here. You understand me boy?" Washington now stood at the front of the stump, in case one of the ropes began to slip off. "Now one, two, pull!" Men heaved against the ropes, their groaning audible all the way up to the plantation's porch. Men on the top of the six foot wide dike struggled as their footing gave way. Men just over the back side of the dike had the slope of the dike's side to push against and leaned their full weight into it. They looked like two rows of Clydesdale horses thrashing against the current of a river. The huge stump leaned forward, groaning and creaking as it fought the men like a stubborn wild stallion who refused to be broken.

"Get in there Leander! Now, I said!" screamed Mordecai.

On the front porch, Graydon Moon was taking his morning tea, a habit he had refused to break even after the Boston Tea Party. He surveyed the rice field and looked across the slaves as a military general might survey his troops.

Leander's eyes were huge and white. He hopped down into the gaping hole, freshly exposed as the stump leaned forward. As he chopped with ferocity against the stubborn roots, the adrenaline exploded in his system causing the rapid motion of the hatchet to blur if one stared directly at it. The men fighting the ropes groaned even louder. Washington's head snapped back and forth, examining the straining ropes wrapped around the stump. Leander thrashed against the roots, his newly sworn enemy, as chunks of wood and debris sprayed in all directions.

12
Entering the Tunnel

"Remmie!" yelled Jupiter, running after the girl. "Wait up!" He turned and looked back once more at the small cypress trees that pointed in the direction they were now running. The woods thickened overhead and darkened once again. It wasn't an ominous place, but instead the forest gave off the feeling of something separate, or more accurately, something *set aside*. The darkness was caused by the density of the pine canopy above. Enormous long-needle and loblolly pine trees lifted up from the forest floor like marble columns supporting a roof of green. The trees were abnormally large and seemed to reach the sky. On the forest floor lay a coating of pine needles so thick a blind person might think he was walking on pillows. No shrubs, no palmettos, no wild blueberry bushes. Remmie stood just ahead, staring up at the monstrous trees. A quiet fell upon the place—there was not a breath of wind, a whistle of air against a bird's wings, not even the familiar drone of mosquitoes buzzing about the ear. Jupiter tip-toed up behind Remmie, almost afraid to make a sound.

Remmie heard him approaching, "Why's it so quiet?" she said.

"I dunno," said Jupiter. "I just ain't never heard it so quiet." His voice trailed off into a whisper.

"And something else," she continued. "You know, I would have thought I'd be scared in a place like this. You know, all dark and as quiet as a ghost? But," she looked about herself then back up at the canopy above, "I'm not. It feels kind of good, doesn't it? Like we're in some kind of a good place."

The further they walked, the more closely the tree trunks seemed to be to one another. The forest was getting denser and began forming into a funnel of tree trunks guiding them closer and closer to some intended path, some preplanned destination. Both looked from side to side, then up and down the tree trunks. Their feet sunk into the pillowing pine needles which yielded under their weight. The funnel narrowed until they stood shoulder to shoulder. It was like being entranced in a kind of special wonder—hazy at the edges, yet brilliantly focused in the center. As they continued their slow walk, the trees caused a curvature in the path as it pushed from one side to the other, waving into a serpentine form. At the end of the serpentine path, the trees, stacked trunk to trunk now, widened and revealed a thatch tunnel with rounded walls so dense, they looked impenetrable.

"I ain't never been in no place like this. What's this tunnel?" said Jupiter. "It smells so good. It smells like...like pine, like fresh split fat-lighter wood. Only, the smell doesn't just go away so quick. It's coming from way down in there somewhere." He pointed deep into the tunnel, then closed his eyes and drew in a deep breath through his nose. "This is something special alright."

"Pine?" quizzed Remmie, "It don't smell anything like pine. It's, it's..." she closed her eyes and inhaled through her nose, her chest rising and falling in the process. "It smells like..."

"Smells like what?" said Jupiter. But when he looked at her, he noticed the flush of her face, and a sudden welling of tears.

Remmie's lip trembled, "Jasmine. It smells like jasmine."

"Remmie? What's wrong? You okay?"

"It's my momma," her voice cracked. "My momma smelled like jasmine. She always did. Least that's how I remember her. It was a perfume Papa got her." Remmie covered her mouth and spun away, ashamed of the tears now streaming.

"Remmie! Remmie, it ain't nuthin'. It's okay Remmie. I, I, I don't even smell it, neither. I just smell pine. That deep, deep smell, like I said, when Daddy splits open a piece of fat-lighter wood, you know, to start a fire with?" His efforts were noble, but they had no effect on Remmie who continued in silent grief. After a moment, she wiped her cheeks and turned back to him.

Then something happened that could never happen in public, not in slave country anyway. Remmie reached out and took Jupiter's hand. He looked behind him as one afraid of being seen, but when she sensed him pull away, she tightened her grip. It was a simple act of friendship, but a strong one—one that gave off the warmth of a fireplace on a blustery night. The two looked down into the tunnel then stepped inside.

The tunnel was constructed in a tapestry of thick vines woven of blackberry stickers, delicate vinca, and muscadine grape. It was so thick that sunlight did not penetrate, yet there was a glow, something in between burnt umber and the yellow of morning's first light. The tunnel seemed to reach forward, gripping the last of several pine trees, as though holding on for its life. It was about seven feet tall at its highest point, and rounded down at the edges into a perfect half circle before burrowing into the ground. Since the tunnel curved off to one side, it was impossible to tell how long it ran by looking down into it.

There was no bedding of pine needles along its floor. Instead, deep, plush moss, as green as spring leaves, formed a sponge-like carpet underfoot, that stretched from one edge to the other.

Jupiter and Remmie's hands gripped tighter against one another, but not out of fear. Instead it was more like *exhilaration*, the way one would feel as they stepped onto the deck of a ship, bound for adventure.

13
Winkles and the Path

The children followed Winkles from the rice field, past the pointing cypress trees, and off into the woods on the trail that Remmie and Jupiter had followed. Lenny wobbled from side to side, shifting his weight back and forth. He looked like a child under the pangs of urgency. Before he could even speak, Mr. Winkles smiled down at him. "Now, Meestah Lenny, what can I help you with? In fact, y'all gather around again. Good, good." Winkles, under the veil of arthritis, dropped to one knee. "Oooh, well, ain't so easy as it used to be, getting down here. So, Lenny, what is in that little noggin of yours?"

"Well," began the boy, "um, um, um, what is this path thing they're on? I don't understand how trees could grow into such a path like this. I mean, you're always wanting us to get down and see nature and stuff, right? I just don't understand. All those big pine trees. It's like they were planted like that, kind of like the perfectly planted cypress trees that formed into the arrow back there."

"Yes, you right about that, Meestah Lenny, you right as rain, you are. Planted, you say? Hmmm, planted. Well, lets all think about this thing. So, we've got all these huge old pine trees and they all seem like they're planted together to make that path." He glanced across at the other children. "Yeah, you're right Lenny, yessirree. And they form a *path*, you say, hmmm, a path. Seems to me that a path is a thing you follow, doesn't it? Yeah, a path. Well, sometimes God has a path for you to follow, and sometimes, he makes it real clear. I'd say you were right, Lenny. Those trees were planted, and they were planted just like that for Miss Remmie, and Mr. Jupiter to follow."

Lenny's eyes blew wide, "You mean God planted those trees way long ago, so they would grow real big, and one day Remmie and Jupiter would walk down it?"

"Y'all all listen here real good. God's not just sitting up there in heaven all day with nothing to do. Nossirree. He's got all kinds of things to do. And most of them, well, most of them are things he's wanting for you. He's like a parent. He's just like your daddy, yessirree. Y'all think about your daddy. He's always looking out for you, and loving you, right?" The children all nodded, with the exception of Lenny. "Now, I know Lenny, I know. Your daddy left a long time ago. I know. But, like I was saying, God has all kinds of plans for you. And sometimes, you just have to walk down that path he laid out."

"My daddy, my daddy left. But he's coming back. He's just got some things he's got to do, that's all." Lenny looked around at the other children and then laid his head into Mr. Winkles chest. Although he didn't utter a sound, the heaving little body spoke volumes of the pain buried within.

"That's alright, Meestah Lenny. It's gonna be alright." Winkles held his pointer finger up to his mouth. The other children knew this was a time to be quiet. "Now, let's look a little more at that tunnel that Remmie and Jupiter are in. So, y'all take a look here at all these vines all twined around to form this tunnel." He put his fingers into the entwined foliage. "We've got a lot'a blackberry vine in here. See? Here's one of the berries now. Lenny, you taste this berry. But if y'all notice, there's muscadine grape vine wrapped all up in here too."

"What's a muk-sadine?" said Lenny, his lips puckering against the not-quite-ripe blackberry he had just eaten.

"Oh!" said Mr. Winkles. "Mus-ca-dine is a vine too. It grows with leaves like this here, and it makes grapes. Let's see, yep, here's one of the grapes. You taste that one little lady," he said, handing the pigtailed little girl the grape. "It got a real thick skin on it, so you might not want to eat the skin, but its gooood, ain't it?"

"Yes, Mr. Winkles," smiled the girl.

"But y'all notice how much blackberry is here compared to muscadine. Ain't much muscadine at all. Most of this here is blackberry, and blackberry's got prickers all over it, yessirree. Poke your finger, it will. Now, these vines didn't just grow out of nowhere. They were planted too. And, like anything else, they have their purpose. In fact, these vines represent something God is wanting to tell us."

Lenny wiped the last evidence of tears from beneath his eyes. "What's he trying to tell us? I mean, it kind of seems mean. Those blackberries are good, but you might get pricked reaching in for one."

"You're exactly right, Lenny, yessirree. These blackberry vines have both sweet and pain all in one, don't they? The sweet berry is something we're all wanting, but sometimes you've got to go through a little pain to get it. Our lives can be like that too. Sometimes the sweetest things in life can be the hardest. And, these blackberry vines are here to remind us of the good and the bad, the light and the dark. See, if there wasn't any dark, well, there couldn't be any light. If there wasn't any light, there'd be nothing but darkness everywhere. The prickers on these vines are the dark, the berries are the light. They're kind of like us. All of us have both good and bad inside us; both light and dark at the same time. It's easy to be bad, and a little harder to be good, but we have light inside us because of what Jesus did for us. Jesus himself is the light, and he's just shining his light all up in the world we live in. But, there's always darkness too."

"So," said Lenny, "if the blackberry vines are light and dark, then what about the muscadine?"

"That's my Lenny," Mr. Winkles said as he laughed. "Well, the muscadine is Jesus *his-self*. See, notice there aren't any prickers on them. They're just pretty leaves and sweet fruit. Jesus ain't got no dark in him at all. And he's the only one. The only, only one who is like that. The rest of us have both the light with the dark."

Lenny walked further into the tunnel, well past the other children. He examined the sides of the tunnel with the scrutiny of a botanist. "Hey, Mr. Winkles, how come there's so much blackberry back there at the entrance, and just a little muscadine, but the further I go down this tunnel, it seems like there's more and more and more muscadine grapes?"

Mr. Winkles knelt down towards the little boy and the other children, "My, my, my. Such a little man, such big questions." He shook his head and smiled, then walked toward the boy. "More muscadine down this way, huh? Hmmm, well, we're gonna have to think about that one, now ain't we?" Winkles rubbed his chin whiskers the way a man might do when steeped in concentration, but the children all knew he already had the answer. "Well, maybe God's trying to tell us something about where this tunnel is going. Seems to me like there are more and more muscadine down this way for a reason. Hmm, yep, he's tryin' to tell us something, yessirree. But what's he trying to say? What did we say the muscadine sweetness was?"

Lenny's hand jutted into the air, straight as a flag pole, "Um, um, um, more and more Jesus?" he blurted.

"Now that's a thought. Yessirree, lets think about that one for a spell. Maybe going down this path is leading us toward more and more *Jesus*," Winkles smile grew as wide as a watermelon at the end of summer. "And to a special place, a special place in-deeeed." Mr. Winkles' laugh infected everyone, and mouths popped open, and smiles abound, and giggles emanated from each of the twelve children as they walked further into the depths of the foliage tunnel.

14
Property Destroyed

Washington stood in front of the massive stump, and concentrated on the ropes as the men pulled. The men behind him stood in two lines, each line fighting against a rope that seemed to have the strength of a Brahma bull. Washington's eyes fixated on the rope on his right as it vibrated under unimaginable tension. At first, the rope just shook, but then, tiny fibers along its surface began to pop. First one, then another, then another. His mind raced. He shook his head back and forth whispering "No, no, no." The rope was about to snap. He leapt into action, yelling something unintelligible to the others, and raced towards Leander, still deep in the stump's pit. With the suddenness of an executioner pulling the lever on the gallows, the rope frayed, and then snapped, sending the men on that side flying backwards. A millisecond later under a double strain, the men on the left rope flung forward, in the direction of the stump, leaving all of them scattered across the mud and dike. In a blur of motion, the stump rocketed back into its original, upright position, punching its full weight towards Leander. There was screaming and the sound of a blood curdling yelp, but the sound cut off before its full potential could be realized. All the slaves scrambled towards the stump, some upright and some scrambling on their hands and knees.

On the porch, Graydon Moon stood straight up with such abruptness that he knocked over his tea tray. All its contents flew into the air, and seemed to hang there for several seconds before crashing to the ground. The imported china teapot, cup and saucer shattered as sharpened shards splayed across the painted wood porch planks scattering in all directions and sliding to a halt. Graydon seemed to not notice the destruction of his tea set but instead stared out in horror at the rice field in the distance. He leapt from the porch, ran past the magnolia trees and crossed out onto the dike.

"My God, my God!" he stammered, "What, what happened?" There, protruding from underneath the stump were the legs of a man. "Oh, oh! Get that man out of there! Get him out of there! Who, who is that?"

Some slaves were around behind the stump trying to pull the man free. Others pulled against the stump with their hands, while the rest grabbed the partial lengths of rope still attached to it. But as they did, their feet dug deeper and deeper into the mud—they had no traction.

The legs were not moving, the torso was fully engulfed under the stump. The scene was one of chaos and pain and acts of panicked heroics all mixed together. The one person not moving was the one most responsible, Mordecai. He stood in the same spot on the dike, staring, and open-mouthed. Thoughts raced through his head. *What have I done? What if he dies? What if he's maimed? Will I have to pay for it? He's a slave, and a slave is property, and I've destroyed property. Will I be thrown off the plantation and have to find work elsewhere?*

"Who, who, who is it?" stuttered Graydon, "Get him out of there! Mordecai! Who is it?"

Mordecai's face was ashen, "It's that older boy. That older boy, Leander." But at that moment, Leander himself wandered from behind the crowd of men with a stunned look on his face.

Graydon scowled at the sight of Leander, then turned on Mordecai the way a dragon might turn towards his next meal. "And who, may I ask, is that?"

Mordecai looked at Leander and went speechless. His right hand trembled as a drop of sweat rolled off his middle finger. He stared at the seventeen-year-old. "I don't understand. I don't understand. You was in the pit. Then who's that? Whose legs is them?" But at this point, he knew. It was Washington. Washington, the most valued slave on the plantation. Washington, the man who engineered the entire system of rice fields, dikes, and gates that operated with the precision of a Swiss grandfather clock. Washington, the slave that three local landowners in the last two years had tried to buy. It was Washington, the father of Jupiter, and he was gone, crushed to death underneath the stump.

Leander stumbled sideways, and in a torrent of adrenaline, blacked out, and fell into the mud. His life having been saved was too much for him. A tall, skinny slave of about fourteen years of age began to cry. He sprinted off into the woods in search of young Jupiter, the boy whose father now lay in ruins.

15
From Blackberry to Muscadine

Remmie pulled Jupiter further down the path. Jupiter's face was blank with wonder. Remmie's mother had died, and the last vestige of Remmie's memory of her was the smell of her jasmine perfume. The stronger the smell became, the harder Remmie pulled, dragging the dazed Jupiter behind her. "Come on, Jupiter, come on! Momma. It's my Momma. She's down here! I just know it. That's her perfume, I can smell it!"

Jupiter shook his head as though waking from a deep sleep. "What are you talking about, Remmie? You know your mama is...," Jupiter stopped himself from saying the word *dead*, but it was too late, Remmie knew what he meant. "I'm sorry, Remmie. I'm sorry."

Remmie stopped in her tracks and looked at him, her bottom lip scrunched under the weight of her top teeth. He hadn't meant it, and she knew it. But, the intoxication enveloping her soul pulled against her heartstrings until the tears, bubbling so near the surface, burst forth. Remmie knew her mother was gone, and wasn't coming back. "I just wanted to see her one more time. I wanted to see her," the words bubbled out in between gasps for air. She wiped her eyes against the ruffled material of her dress. "Let's just keep going. Seems like this vine tunnel is meant for us to follow, you know?"

"Yeah, okay," replied the boy, still smarting under the pain of his friend's trampled feelings.

As the two continued, the change from blackberry sticker vines to muscadine was more apparent than ever. The number of ripe muscadine grapes, dangling above their heads, intensified. As they neared what looked like the end of the tunnel, the entire ceiling above them was awash with purple grapes, dark and waxy. The increasing glow of light penetrating the ceiling passed through the grapes and cast a hue of blue-purple across everything.

"Look! Look up there!" said Jupiter.

Remmie's mouth went wide, "Ooooooohhhhh!"

Before them was a glow of light, so golden, it looked as though the air itself radiated in the precious metal. The light shone from all directions, and bathed everything around it in warmth. The tunnel opened wide, and this new space in front of them seemed to have no beginning and no end.

Inside the enormous space stood an object of about fourteen feet in height, far taller than the edge of the tunnel where they stood. The object was hard to focus on, and the harder they stared at it, the less focused it became. They stood at the edge of the massive space and looked at each other. The golden light draped across them and painted their skin with the weight of a silk robe— soft, buttery, yet as solid as fabric.

Neither knew what to say. It was as though all of their thoughts and fears had retreated to that place in your mind where worries go after they've been beaten back, too far away to hurt you any more.

"I feel like I'm floating," said Remmie, "like something in a dream. You know, like when you're in a dream and you're flying?"

But Jupiter was too fixated on the object. "What is it?" he said, cocking his head to the side. "I can't hardly see it."

"I know," said Remmie as she turned her attention forward and rubbed her eyes. "How come it's so fuzzy looking?"

"I can't see," said Jupiter. "It's all messy. My eyes, they can't see it." His chest began a steady heave, up and down. "Remmie, I'm getting scared. What's wrong with my eyes..."

"Don't be scared Jupiter. It'll be okay, it'll be okay." She redoubled her efforts to focus on the object. After a few moments, she said, "Oh, wait." She was quiet at first. "Wait, wait," her tempo began to increase, "I can see it! I can see it," she said, as excited as a ten-year-old girl hyped up on sugar. "Don't look so hard! Don't look so hard at it, see? Look like, look like you're looking *past* it."

As Jupiter relaxed his eyes, the edges of the object became clearer until finally it came into crisp focus. Remmie leaned her torso forward, yet her feet stayed planted to the ground. She peered into the space, looking from side to side. It wasn't until they stepped fully out of the tunnel and into the opening, that the golden glow began its slow retreat, leaving in its wake, clear, daylight. They watched with gaping mouths as the thick, liquid gold glow seeped upwards, back into the structure of the dome-shaped room. The dome was high, and woven entirely of grape vines that seemed to permeate its entire surface. The ceiling came into visibility and stood perhaps forty feet in height.

Both children looked back at the object before them, sharp and crisp. It was a series of brown, interwoven vines that were formed into the shape of the base of a large oak tree. There was enough space between the vines to see into the hollow cavity that they created, and straight through to the other side of the room. The vines were heavy at the base, and thinned as they grew upwards. To the children it appeared that the vines had grown up from the ground, surrounded the trunk of a huge live oak tree, yet the tree was no longer there. Dotted across some of the vines were delicate, spring-green leaves, all clustered in groups of three.

Jupiter spoke first, "I seen something like this once."

"What is it?"

"I can't remember it much. But a long time ago, me and my momma were walking in the woods." Jupiter closed his eyes and the scene painted itself onto his mind's eye. "We saw something just like this here. It was a bunch of vines that growed up around a tree. Must have taken years and years. And then, the tree must have died because there wasn't nothing left of the tree any more, except maybe some bark an stuff. And even though the tree had died, the vines just were still standing there, still in the shape they had grown around that tree."

Remmie tiptoed forward and looked across it in marvel. With the gentleness of a child petting a newborn lamb, she extended her hand to feel the vines' polished thickness. But before her fingers reached the surface, Jupiter snatched her hand, yanking it back. She startled, and looked at him.

"Poison ivy," he said.

"Poison...?" But as she looked closer, she realized he was right.

"Three leaves," he said as he pointed to their jagged asymmetry.

They walked in different directions around the hulk of hollow vines and looked up and down its shape. It was the perfect replica of the trunk of a live oak tree, right down to the way it sprawled wide at the base, forming the telltale structure. As they continued around it, first Remmie, then Jupiter stopped. On the other side was an opening in the shape of an archway that led into the center of the vine tree. They looked at one another. The archway stood around seven feet tall, around the same height as the serpentine tunnel that led them here.

"Wow," quipped Remmie, "did you just see that?"

"See what?"

"Those vines, those poison ivy vines, did you see up at the top?" She pointed towards the highest point of the archway. "The vines, they were moving, growing up to the top." Remmie's fear arced inside her and stabbed at her lungs, but she shut her eyes tight and squeezed it back down.

"Growing? Them vines ain't growing Remmie. You're seeing things."

"No, no, it was, I swear it. It looked like..." Remmie withdrew her hand from the air and looked all around the room.

"Like what?"

"Like it finished growing into place right as we got here. Right as we walked around this side." Then she said something that they were both thinking. "Do you think we should go inside it?"

But before Jupiter could answer, something flickered on the ground in front of them. It looked like a flash of light, brilliantly bright, but it didn't hurt to look into. The shape of the light formed into the outline of a walkway and was gone as fast as it had appeared. They both stood in stunned silence, afraid the other had not seen it. Neither spoke, neither flinched, neither breathed—they were waiting for whatever might happen next. As their eyes struggled to grasp what they had just seen, Jupiter could hold it in no longer, "Remmie," he said, putting his hand over his mouth, "did you see that? It looked like a pathway, didn't it? It looked like a brick pathway, and the bricks were made of," he was almost afraid to say the word, "gold."

Remmie made not a sound. Her breath eased in, then out, in, then out. All the while, tears rose against her eyes, as she struggled both to hold them in abatement, and to grasp the vision of the golden path that had just flashed before her. The invisible barrier she had built to fight the tears began a steady crumble, much like the way a sandcastle capitulates to the relentless pounding of ocean waves. In the end, there was one overriding factor she could not control. It was the enchanting aroma, the aroma of her mother's jasmine perfume, a fresh haunting that after the long struggle won out. To Remmie, if the holy spirit had a smell, this was it.

Faint memories of her beautiful mother flashed before her, then rolled away, disappearing into the distance. And like waves of raindrops in a spring gale, tears poked out, just a few at first, then in a steady pattern, and finally a torrent.

Although Jupiter could not smell the jasmine, he knew what it meant to her. And in the tenderness that can only be experience by true friends, he took a step towards Remmie, leaned his head on her shoulder, and held her tight around the waist. Not a word was said, but soon her low sobbing put a choke-hold on his throat, and tears rolled from his eyes as well.

And that's the way they stayed—standing with resolute anticipation of the journey that lay before them. Both knew they must step into the hollow poison ivy tree even though they did not know why.

Several minutes passed before the glow started again. At first, it was barely visible, but then climbed in intensity until it was undeniable. The ground in front of them, and just under their feet, emanated the same hue of yellow gold they had seen a few minutes before. The color illuminated them from below, and painted their clothing, and faces in brilliant light. It penetrated through several inches of thick green moss that carpeted the undersides of their hard-soles shoes. Then the moss converted into a physical structure, both solid and flat. Symmetrical lines formed down the long axis of the newly flattened surface, followed by cross-hatches that appeared in between the longer lines. They were witnessing the formation of a brick pathway, a pathway paved in gold. The tears stopped, and the children stared, and all was quiet, lest the beating of two hearts that pumped in unison.

16
A Neat, Structured List

The twelve children stood aghast at the magic they were witnessing. They lined the circular thatch wall of muscadine and stood in silence, fearing that if they moved, Remmie and Jupiter would see them. Mr. Winkles stood in the middle of the small group, a child's small hand in each of his. He looked first to his left, then to his right, and gazed into their very souls with eyes of warmth and love. He looked at their little mouths, many of which hung open, he looked at their eyes, rounded and glazed, and he smiled.

Winkles reached out and touched Lenny's shoulder, then helped himself down onto one knee, knowing the time was soon that Remmie and Jupiter would step into the center of the poison-ivy tree. Once they did, they would disappear and enter a place like no other—no other *on earth* that is. Once that happened, the questions would proliferate and he would once again be called upon to explain what was happening, and more importantly, its meaning.

Lenny leaned against Mr. Winkles, and his hands crunched into the old man's frayed sweater. His little mind captured every detail, every word spoken, and as he did, questions formed in his mind and ordered themselves into a neat, structured list.

17
Silent Liquid Light

Remmie and Jupiter took each other by the hand, turned, and without further hesitation, stepped through the archway and inside the poison ivy tree. As they stopped in its center, an eruption of silent, liquid light befell them from above. Had the light moved slower, it might have appeared to move the way the flowing of molten lava engulfs whatever is in its path. This light was not hot, however, but instead emanated a clean warmth, more akin to the warmth of a heart that is filled with love. As the liquid filled the hollow tree trunk, it arced in a single flash of light, and was gone.

18
The Vanishing

Lenny gasped as he realized Remmie and Jupiter were no longer standing where they once had. But when he turned to Mr. Winkles to unleash his torrent of questions, he caught his own reflection in Winkles' eye, and with that, found they no longer stood in the rounded muscadine room, but were once again in the woods, near the opening of the tunnel.

Lenny's questions overwhelmed him, and he took no notice of his new surroundings. Both of Lenny's hands yanked up and down on the grayed fabric of Mr. Winkles' old sweater, and Winkles began a slow, steady laugh. Lenny's mind raced, and his list of prioritized questions became jumbled, one falling before the other, and others mixing the front half of one question with back half of another.

"Um, um, um, um," stammered the boy.

"That's alright Meestah Lenny, that's alllll-right. You just take a deep breath, and it'll come, yessirree. It'll come."

Lenny re-collected his thoughts, but his mouth had yet to catch up, "Where, where, where'd they go? Are they alright? I don't understand."

"Yes, yes, I know, I know." He passed his crinkled fingers over Lenny's head. "Y'all all circle around to old Mr. Winkles, and we gonna talk about this thing. There's a lot we just saw, ain't it? Yessirree, a lot." Winkles drew in a deep breath. "So, why don't we start in the smartest place—we're gonna start right where we left off, when little Remmie and little Jupiter went into this tunnel of vines and such. Now, we already talked about what the sticker blackberries were about, and what the pretty muscadine grapes were. But, anybody noticehow this tunnel curves back and forth, swirling from one way to the next?"

The little girl's timidity almost got the best of her, but she stepped towards the grandfather. "I did. I remember it. The tunnel swishes back and forth as you walk down it. I didn't think it was hardly anything to notice, but they had a word for it. Um, it was ser-pen-time."

Winkle's head leaned back as he contained his laughter, "You just right as rain, little Missy, you right as rain. You're right, there's a word for it. It's ser-pen-teen. Serpentine. Now, who knows what that word means?" He looked at each child in turn.

Lenny's hand shot into the air, "Ooo, ooo, ooo, I know, I know!" he said as his feet ran in place. "It means, um, um, it means something like a snake."

"Yessirree, you're right about that, Lenny. That word serpentine means in the shape of a snake." He surveyed the quizzical faces. "Now, if this whole tunnel thing has all this stuff about Jesus in it, you know, like how the grapes are sweet and good just like Jesus, then what's this snake got to do with it?" The last few words rolled off his tongue as fast as a snapping turtle strikes.

The children's heads did not turn, but their eyes darted back and forth at each other.

"Who remembers Adam and Eve? I bet y'all all remember them. And what happens in the garden with Adam and Eve?"

Lenny glanced at his classmates, then back at Winkles. "Oooo, yeah. In the garden, there's a snake, and, it told Eve to eat the apple, right?"

"You right as rain, Meestah Lenny, yessirree. In the Garden of Eden, a serpent told Eve that it's okay to eat an apple that God told her not to eat." He spoke in the justified tone of a mother scolding a child. "Yessirree, that serpent lied to Miss Eve, and she believed him. When she ate the apple, that's what they call *original sin* because that's the first time anybody sinned against God. But, y'all know what? There's not a one of us who has ever been born that wasn't going to sin. Nossirree, not one. Every one of us is gonna sin. We just aren't perfect. And if you think about it, Eve eating that apple almost doesn't matter, does it?"

"But why not," cried Lenny. "If she hadn't eaten the apple, everything would have been alright."

"Well," said Mr. Winkles, "maybe so, Meestah Lenny, maybe so. But, the next person to be born would have sinned, right? Because there isn't anybody that's perfect, right? So, all us humans, wandering around down here would have sinned, and sin is what separates us from God, and that's what makes him sad. So see, Eve doing that o-riginal sin isn't the point. No, it's not the point at all. The point of the story of the Garden of Eden is that we humans are not perfect, and that means we're gonna separate ourselves from God. We just can't help it."

Lenny's head turned upwards looking at Winkles, and he tugged on his sweater, "The ser-teen tunnel, what about the ser-teen tunnel?"

"Oh! Well see, this tunnel is shaped like a serpentine, isn't it? The serpentine is like sin. We walked down the tunnel. The tunnel represents the fact that we all walk in sin. Even as we walk with Jesus, we walk in sin. But lets think about where this tunnel is taking Jupiter an Remmie. What's down at the end of this tunnel of sin?"

"Poison ivy!" blurted the little girl, laughing at her own boldness.

The children laughed but settled quickly.

Mr. Winkles turned towards her, "The poison ivy, well, yes little Missy. And ain't that strange. Ain't it strange that the hollow tree of vines is made up of *poison* ivy. And it's standing in the center of that big place that's just covered up in muscadine grapes. There's so many of them that the whole place is almost purple with them. That place is covered up in Jesus, right? Yessirree, that's a tough one, ain't it? But let's figure on this thing. Let me ask y'all a question. Does anybody remember the story about a man walking down the road, and meeting Jesus himself? Anybody know it? This is the man that was real mean, real bad. Anybody remember it now? Well, alright, y'all just take a seat. That's right, y'all sit down, criss cross applesauce."

As the children sat in front of Mr. Winkles, he shifted from one knee to the other, the arthritis was getting the best of him.

"Once upon a time, there was this man, named by his momma as Sssss-aul. Now Saul was, well, he was a bad man, yessirree. See, this was around the time that Jesus was walking the earth, telling the good news! But then, as y'all know, Jesus died and went to heaven." Winkles rocked straight up, "But before then, Saul, didn't like Jesus a'tall, nossirree. He was always going around and being mean to folks that followed Jesus, and he was doing bad things. Well, one day, Saul was walking all by his lonesome out on a country road. So Saul's all alone, and who walks up to him but Jesus himself! Yessirree, and Jesus made something happen to Saul that changed Saul forever."

"Did he hurt him?" whispered the pigtailed girl.

"Oh, no, Missy. Jesus doesn't wanna hurt anybody. No, Jesus did something that changed Saul forever. He healed his heart. See Saul's heart was so filled with dirt and meanness that he needed help, and Jesus helped him. After that, Saul's heart was so changed, even his name was changed. He was now named Paul, and Paul went out, and spread the good word like nobody's business. It's kind of like this poison ivy vine. See, a long time ago, there was a big old oak tree, and around it grew a little bitty vine of poison ivy. Well, that poison ivy grew and grew. Kind of like y'all are doing."

Lenny leaned in, "My grandma says that. Every time I see her, she says how much I've grown. What's she think I'm going to do, shrink?"

Winkles laughed, "You're right Lenny, yessirree. So, after a while, the poison ivy grew all around that tree and choked it. The oak tree died. It's kind of like Saul, isn't it? See Saul's own heart was choked by all his hatred of the people following Jesus. Finally, with help from Jesus, himself, the old Saul died. Not the man, but the badness in his heart. The badness died, and what was left was just the goodness. This poison ivy is the new Paul that came out of that road with a healed heart."

"But, but, but, but," said Lenny, "why is it *poison* ivy? Why isn't it just some nice ivy? You know, like the kind that doesn't itch any."

"Well, Meestah Lenny, the poison ivy is kind of something that is untouchable, isn't it? It's to remind us that unless you go through Jesus, the Father himself is untouchable—you can't get to him without going through the son. The father wants to talk to you. He wants to talk to all of you. And that's why he sent Jesus to us. So we can talk to God himself." He surveyed the young faces to make sure they were tracking, and then added, "Since all us have so much sin, Jesus balanced all that out by giving up His life. It was like a payment, a payment he made for something he didn't owe. He was paying it for us because he loves us."

Lenny looked at his shoes. "But he doesn't even know us. He died because of something we did?"

The grandfather looked at Lenny hard, "It's deeper than that, son. It's...more personal than that. You see, it not because of something we did. It's because of each person, each one of us is full of sin. He died to even out the sin, in me, and...in you."

Lenny thought on that a moment. Then Mr. Winkles said, "It doesn't matter what we did, either. It doesn't matter if we are the worst of the worst, or if we just maybe did something real small."

"That doesn't seem fair," said Lenny. "How come if we did something real bad, it's the same as somebody that barely did anything at all?"

Winkles looked up to the tops of the pine trees, "Hmmm, let me think on how I can es-plain it to you. Alright, I've got a question. Anybody ever been on a trip and been on an airplane?"

Several hands shot into the air, including Lenny's. "You've been on an airplane there little man? Where'd you go?"

"Oh, oh, we went to Florida...me and Daddy and Momma...." Lenny stopped with the suddenness of a car slamming a brick wall. The sting of the loss of his own father raw, and fresh. He buried his head into Mr. Winkles.

"That's alright, little man, that's alright. You just let it all go." The loss of his father was something Lenny carried close to the surface at all times. After a few moments, Mr. Winkles continued. "Y'all lean in here and listen real close, because there's something I need to tell you, and I want you all to remember it. Think about it this way. Let's say y'all have gone to the airport to get on to the airplane. Only thing is, you were late. Your airplane supposed to leave at a certain time, and you were late. You get there, and the plane has gone because you were late by two minutes." The kids all looked at one another. "Then, while you're sitting there for a while, all upset about missing your plane, and how you ain't gonna get where you were goin', and how you ain't gonna get no Biscotti cookies on the plane, and then another person runs up, and they're supposed to be on that plane too. The only thing is, they were *twenty* minutes late." He looked at them to see who was catching on. "See, it doesn't matter if you were two minutes late, or twenty minutes late, you missed your plane either way, right? That's what sin is like. Sin has a cost to it, and it has to be paid whether it's big sin or tiny sin. It's still got to be paid, and it doesn't matter if you was the only person on the whole world, and you done sinned just a little bit. Sin is an imbalance in the way things are supposed to be, just like darkness is an imbalance too. We need the light to balance out the dark. With sin, Jesus is the only one who can make it right, and giving up his life is the only way to even things out again.

"See when it's our time to leave this earth, we're gonna walk down this serpentine tunnel, walking through our sin that we did. And we're gonna walk into that poison ivy tree and be washed in beautiful light. You know what's in that light? Well, Mr. Winkles is gonna tell you. *Forgiveness* is in there. Forgiveness and grace. That light washes us all clean. There isn't any sin it can't clean."

"I don't see any water or anything," said the pigtails. "How are we going to get clean with just a bunch of light?"

Winkles laughed then tweaked her nose with his thumb and forefinger.

"It's like this, little Missy. It's kind of like being in a dark, dark room. Y'all know what I mean? Maybe you remember some dark night, with a big storm outside, and it's all scary. And maybe you went and hid in your closet. Well, if you had a flashlight or a lantern like we used to have, and you turn it on, that light cuts through the dark, doesn't it." Kids nodded their heads up and down in unison. "The fact is, there's no kind of dark that a flashlight can't cut through. See, Jesus *himself* is light. He'll always be light, and there's no sin his light can't cut through."

Lenny's chest began to heave up and down, and his cheeks flushed crimson. He was holding something inside that wanted in desperation to escape.

"Are you sure, Mr. Winkles?" he said as his voice cracked. "Are you sure big sin isn't more important than little sin?"

Mr. Winkles picked him up and sat him on his lap, then scratched the curly gray whiskers under his own chin. He then put his hand on Lenny's chest, and pressed against it to feel the beating of Lenny's heart.

"I knew this time was coming little man, I knew. It's something inside you, isn't it? Something covering your heart, and it's eating your insides, isn't it?"

A tear bulged, and then made a hasty escape, rolling underneath Lenny's glasses then down his cheek.

"Don't you worry about those tears, Lenny. Tears are something that form inside us before we can even see them. Tears can't be stifled for long, and once they're formed, they got to find their way out, one way or another. And it's best to just let them out." He pulled Lenny's head onto his shoulder and held the boy. "I'll tell y'all children something, something I've never told anybody. I've got me a gift," he looked around at each child. "I do, yessirree. When I was just a little boy, Jesus gave me a gift, just sure as you're born, he did. He gave me one gift, and he gave my best friend another gift."

Before he could continue, the little girl blurted out, "What was it, Mr. Winkles? Was it a stuffed animal, like a bunny? Was it a puppy? Was it..."

Winkles lay back, again infecting the kids with his laughter.

"Hold on there little Missy, hold on now. No, it wasn't a puppy, nor a stuffed bunny rabbit. But those are fine gifts, fiiiiiine gifts indeed. No, my gift was different. I'll have to tell you about it sometime. But, the gift I want to tell y'all about is the gift he gave my friend. Jesus gave her something that she carries deep down inside. He gave her a way to see just a little bit of the way *he* can see. He gave her a way to see deep into a person's heart, and see if their heart is sad, or happy, or mean or sweet. Sweet as Fanny's homemade pumpkin pie. You know how Fanny does it, with that sweet crème she whips up in a bowl, and puts on top of the pie? Um, mmm, yessirree. Oh, sorry. Y'all ain't had Fanny's homemade pumpkin pie."

As if they were alive, giggles started with the pigtails, and then traveled to her left and continued around the circle of children jumping from one to the next, until they were satisfied.

"I got carried away thinking about Fanny's pumpkin pie. Anyway, God gave my best friend this gift so that when she looks at you, she can see your heart. I can't see it, but she kind of taught me how to *feel*, yessirree. Lenny, that heart of yours; its got more than just a heartbeat. It's got a feel, and it's got a color too. Yep, sure as you're born, it's got a color. When you're sad, your heart has the color of a pumpkin that's started to rot. Yessirree, kind of dark orange with a little bit of brown in it. And if you're happy, your heart has the color of fresh new leaves on that maple tree over yonder, just as purty as can be. A real purty green with some yellow mixed in. And there's more too. See, your heart isn't just happy and sad, your heart can also show two other colors; two colors for things that are real important to God himself."

The children leaned in closer, as though afraid they wouldn't hear the words.

He cupped his hand to his mouth, and whispered, "Righteousness and wickedness. That's right, your heart can be righteous, or wicked, and most times, there's a little bit of both in there at the same time. Question is, how much righteousness is in there so as to be stronger than the wickedness? If your heart has lots and lots a righteousness in there, it's full of what I call *the shining* colors. All the shining colors are like the colors of these purty trees, and leaves, and the blooms on those azalea bushes over yonder, and the morning sunshine—all the goodness in the world." His smile widened as if he was pulling it with his fingers, then he let it retreat. "Any color of the rainbow, too. Those are shining colors. Then, there's the other side. There's got to be a balance, right? If your heart is all poisoned with wickedness, it's got all the colors of darkness. Sometimes, if a heart is too filled with wickedness, the color is all dark, like a turnip that dried up, or a log that fell over on the ground and rotted. Maybe, sometimes there's just a tiny bit of shining color in it, so you see a bit of the purple, like what you see in the sky at dusk. That means that somewhere deep down inside, that heart has just a bit of righteousness in it, but that righteousness can't get out because there's too much dark in there. Y'all understand?"

None of the children nodded, as they were all lost in thought, but no affirmation was really needed.

"So God gave my friend this gift of seeing the colors, and a gift from God is something he's meaning for you to use." He flattened his hand onto Lenny's chest once again. "Lenny, I ain't really got to touch you like this to know you've got something weighing on your heart. I can feel your heart, little man, and it's a beautiful thing. My friend would say it's as purty as she ever saw. And she'd be telling me it's the color of that red you see sometimes at night, you know? Like here near the ocean when they're talking about, *red sky at night, sailors de-light?* It means if the sky is red at dusk, it's going to be a purty day in the morning. But, Lenny, your heart has something lying over the top of it, kind of covering it up. Kind of like...well like this musty old blanket my grandmamma used to have. That old blanket, all musty smelling and full a moth holes and such, and she wouldn't get rid of it, nossirree. She wouldn't get rid of it. But you, Meestah Lenny, you're carrying something like that around with you too. Don't you think it's time to let it outta there?"

"I'm scared," whispered the boy.

"You're with friends now, yessirree. Whatever it is, you're with friends now and it's gonna be okay."

"I did something, something a long time ago." Tears rolled down his face but his voice was stoic, solid.

"Ain't nothing you done too big for Jesus."

"It was my daddy. He was sleeping, and, and, and he told me to wake him up when the little hand was on the three, and the big hand was on the twelve. He, he, he was sleeping and I was supposed to wake him up! And, I, I forgot. And then when I remembered I went and shook him, but he...," his voice broke apart, "he wouldn't move, and, and, he was all cold-like, and I kept shaking him, and the more I shook the more I got scared. I covered him up with the blankets to get him warm, but it wouldn't do any good." His mouth pursed and his eyes shut and a floodwater of tears plotted down and dotted Mr. Winkles sweater, soaking into the old cloth.

"That's when your daddy died? That was it?"

Lenny nodded his head up and down.

"And, you're thinking that it was your fault, that your daddy died, don't cha?"

Lenny again nodded. "If I'd have just waked him up when the little hand was on the three and the big hand was on the...."

Winkles held his head high into the air. "Now you look-a here. Ain't nobody's fault that your daddy died, you hear me? Especially not yours. Ain't your fault a-tall, no sir. Nossirree.

"But the big hand was on the..."

"Ain't no matter little man. Ain't no matter what time it was. It ain't your fault your daddy died. You could have woke him up or not woke him up, it was just his time," the vowel sound in the word *time* stretched out like an ostrich's neck. "We don't get to choose our time. When it comes, it comes, and there's not anything you or anybody can do about it."

Lenny's breathing began to quiet.

"And I wish I could tell you why it was his time, but I can't. God didn't give me that gift. You know, sometimes, maybe God needs that person in heaven real, real bad. Maybe there's a whole bunch'a children up in heaven that needs a daddy real, real bad. I don't know. Or maybe God doesn't get all in the way of everything happening down here, but instead lets a whole lotta things just happen as they will, then after that, he tries to use whatever happens for his own purpose. I just don't know. But lets take a look-see," he leaned back to peer at Lenny's chest once again, "Yeah, I think my friend would be telling me that old blanket is starting to fall off your heart, yessirree. It might take little while, but I think you now know it wasn't your fault, and there's no more sense carrying that old blanket around any more."

"Mr. Winkles?" inquired the pigtails.

"Yes, sweet pea."

"What's your gift? The one God gave you. You told us you could feel a little bit of what your friend could see in a person's heart. But I get the feeling that's not the gift you were talking about."

"Oh, well, we gonna talk about that later."

19
The Purring of the Birds

Even the red, sunburned neck of Mordecai looked pale and clammy. He walked away from the scene and across the dike as though his joints had stiffened. Even his arms didn't swing normally, and his eyes glazed in a thick, eggshell-like coating. And although his movements were slow, his mind raced. *I'm going to be blamed, I'm going to lose my job, I'm going to have to repay the price of that slave. Washington was no average slave, he was the only reason the plantation was able to enter the rice trade in the first place. He was young, strong, and easily worth $1,500, maybe as high as $1,700, a price recently offered for him. I'll never be able to work in the county again...I'll have to move away...*

No one noticed his slow retreat—they were too focused on trying to pry up the stump and pull Washington's body free. Only two people, the plantation owner, Graydon Moon, and one other slave driver, focused on Leander, the slave boy who still lay unconscious. At this point, it was hard to tell if Leander had simply fainted after having been knocked clear of the falling stump, or if he'd been knocked unconscious and perhaps would die.

"Well is he going to die too?" questioned Graydon. "I can't believe that fool Mordecai! Washington is...was the most valued slave in my possession. How do you think this dike system was engineered! You fools!"

"Sir...I, I ain't..." stammered the other slave driver. "I done told Mordecai...I, he shouldn't'a done this. He...I told him the only way to do it was to hitch up the horse teams and get to pullin'...but he's as hardheaded as a mule."

"I ought to have *him* horse whipped! And Washington, oh my God. And Maxwell Prayer offered me near seventeen hundred dollars for him not four weeks ago. Mordecai will be paying me for the loss of my property."

Graydon Moon looked down at the polished black leather of his shoes, now caked in light brown mud that had previously never even graced the soles.

"And his boy," said Graydon. "Washington has that little boy. What's his name?"

The other man stuttered, "Uh, uh, Jupiter. His name is Jupiter, sir."

"Well someone needs to tell him his father is dead. He'll have to live with someone else. Not even old enough to do anything besides carry water, darn sure not old enough to sell for anything."

"That other boy, he done ran off into the woods to find 'im."

"And I better not find my daughter is with him again. If it kills me, I'll teach her her place."

"Yassir"

"And where the hell is Mordecai? This job isn't over! I want this mess cleaned up! I want this field ready for planting and flooding by morning. I'm not going to delay a rice harvest because of some darned fool slave driver who doesn't respect his employer. If we don't get the seed in the ground, we'll never get a crop. Now get this field ready."

"Yassir, they're gonna work on it....they's gettin' the body out..."

Graydon pointed a sharp finger in the man's face. "He was worth a fortune to me alive. But he's worth nothing to me dead. Getting the body out is none of my concern. I don't care if it is removed or not." He stepped closer, "This field will be planted in rice and flooded tomorrow, or you'll find yourself seeking new employment as well."

When Remmie and Jupiter opened their eyes they found themselves in an embrace they could not recall initiating, and it startled them. They were the best of friends, but to be found holding hands, a plantation owner's child and a slave, much less embracing, would spell trouble the likes of which neither wanted to envision. No, they had to remain vigilant to keep their friendship more secretive than they once had. Graydon Moon had told his daughter to stay away from the other slave children; that she was 'above their station,' and as such could not interact with them.

Remmie had railed against her father at first, but later that night, the house slave, Fanny, had sat her down and told her it would be better to agree with her father, but visit with Jupiter quietly, and out of sight. It was the only solution.

Both children pulled apart with the social awkwardness befalling their friendship, and looked around themselves in an attempt to obtain their bearings.

"What happened, Remmie? We stepped into that poison ivy tree, and, and, all that light came all around, and now we're...we're...where are we?"

"It's so beautiful," replied the girl. "I've never seen anything so beautiful, except maybe my momma."

The sounds of birds chirping surrounded them, but there was a harmony about it. Instead of the random sounds from birds in the forest, it was almost as if the chirping formed into a cadence. It was slow at first, then the tempo increased, and a song ushered out. It was music, and it was unmistakable. It was formed from many different species of birds, all singing in one cohesive effort. The volume rose, then fell, and the song repeated a chorus that had been heard moments before.

"Them birds are singing Remmie!. Listen! I've never heard no birds all singing together in one song. What is this place?"

"Some kind of magic place," mumbled Remmie, as though she were speaking to a ghost. "Where's that coming from?"

"Got to be from over that way," said Jupiter, walking in the direction of the chorus.

They walked through an elaborate forest and gawked at the size of the trees, the color of the leaves, the freshness of the smell; like pure springtime after a rain shower—and the vibrancy of the color. But it wasn't what Remmie could smell that she noticed, it was what she couldn't. Her mother's jasmine; the intoxicating scent of her mother's jasmine perfume had disappeared. She had thought the reason she had been led to this place had to do with her mother. She had hoped it was to *see* her mother, though she knew that was impossible. The noticeable absence of perfume sent a rock into the pit of her stomach, w attention.

They continued down a well trodden trail, the edges of which were bordered with tumbled river stone, as smooth and rounded as they'd ever seen. Each stone was buried half way into the earth, and served to contain the thick bedding of purple flower petals piled deep onto the path. The petals were comprised entirely from wisteria blooms that dangled above their heads in strong concentration. Remmie marveled at the loose flower petals as they shuffled off the tops of her shoes, and wondered why they didn't blow around in the breeze. Outside of the path, the ground was a carpet of fresh, long-needle pine straw, the color of which reminded her of Fanny's sweet tea.

Jupiter's experience was similar to Remmie's, but different at the same time. "Look up at the sky!" exclaimed Jupiter. He gawked with the awe only a child lost in discovery can experience. "That sky...its soooo pretty." The blues in the sky blended from lighter to deeper and intermixed with the slightest hint of green and yellow. The effect was similar to the mix of colors in the Caribbean ocean. "Look at all the stars in the sky! I ain't *never* seen no stars in the daylight! Hey...you can smell it though, can't you?" He closed his eyes and drew in a deep breath through his nose. "Yessirree, fresh split fat lighter. It smells just like if my daddy was right here, splitting it. And, and, I'm smelling me some ham hocks and cornbread, just like Fanny makes. Um, hmm, smells mighty good."

"Jupiter, what are you talking about? I can't smell ham hocks or lighter wood or none of that. And what stars in the sky? I don't see any stars."

But Jupiter's smile was unabated, "Come on!" he said, as he scurried down the winding path. "There's got to be something cooking down this here way!"

"Jupiter! No! Where are you going? Wait!" But it was too late; the boy rounded the next bend in the path and was gone. For the first time, fear crept into Remmie's stomach, and began a steady crawl upwards, infusing her lungs like soot from a cigarette. But before it could take hold, another breeze ushered across her face and caused her golden hair to dance. Behind the breeze came a glow, like moonlight shimmering off a pond at night. And, riding on the glow was a sound of such pure harmony that the fear wisped away as though carried by dozens of little fingers. The harmony approached her from the front, and wrapped around her, circling left, then right. Remmie smiled, but as the feeling penetrated into her heart she started to laugh. She closed her eyes, laid her head back and spun round and round and round, arms extended into the light. And as the feeling in her heart intensified, she felt a flutter, then a steady beating inside her chest. If felt as though a second heart lay atop the first, and beat in unison with it.

She stood basking in the mixture of feelings, and soaked in the sounds of birds whose music built higher and higher reaching a crescendo. Though she wanted to open her eyes and look around, she held them closed. The breeze ebbed and flowed like the breath of a person, and she realized, with startling clarity, that the feeling in her chest wasn't just the presence of a second, overlaying heartbeat, it was the *absence* of every last vestige of pain, worry, fear, heartache, sadness, and loss. The problem was, the wonderful feeling pressing into her heart could only penetrate into the outer layers. It pushed and pushed, trying to get in, but for some reason, remained blocked. The part that had penetrated felt like it was trying to abate a weight from her chest that she hadn't even comprehended was there. Yet the more she basked in the feather-like feelings, the more she realized the weight had always been there, at least as long as she could remember. The more she realized this, the more pronounced was her understanding of just how heavy her heart had become.

Peeking through one eye, then cracking the other, her vision flooded with motion from what must have been thousands of tropical birds lining the forest floor. Their colors swirled and popped from every angle. The breeze on her face had been produced by their wings as they swayed back and forth, like men on a ship in high seas. The music they produced ebbed and flowed as the chorus once again, took over.

Watching the birds was intoxicating. They seemed to be paying attention to nothing specific, yet all sang in a harmony that could not be explained. Like other things she had seen on this day, their magic was something Remmie just had to accept. She immersed herself into the moment and tried to memorize the scene, its every detail, its every facet. And she paid particular attention to the floating feeling surrounding her heart—it became the center of her focus, and she could no longer ignore it.

Dozens of birds, those with the longest feathers, fluttered off the ground and hovered in front of her in two groups. Their bodies were a shimmering azure mixed with speckled green, and their wings, with feathers as long as her hair, were translucent red. They paused in mid flight and seemed to look her in the eye. Remmie would later recall that they were smiling, the birds were actually smiling. She felt more exhilarated and yet more at peace than any time she could remember.

The birds landed on her extended arms with the gentleness of a breeze touching a dandelion. At first she thought their claws might hurt, but instead, she was greeted with a tingling sensation that could best be described as the feeling of being tickled by her father just before bedtime. That was something that had stopped on the night her mother died, and never returned.

Old memories flooded over her, only instead playing out in her head, they played out before her eyes. Her mother playing games to get her to eat peas, Fanny singing to stop her crying after a skinned knee, the joy of that wooden rocking horse she received one Christmas morning. As each memory appeared, the scenery around her changed. It was unlike any experience she had ever had. Some scenes flickered by with the speed of a fish striking a worm, while others played out in real-time. It wasn't until one memory surfaced did the smile leave her face. Although the feeling of elation still swirled around her, the sadness of what that one memory meant punched through with vigor, as tears welled, then streamed down her face. It was the vision of the newel cap.

The memory was of one particular day. On that day Washington's hand-carved newel post and cap had been installed at the bottom of the stair banister in the plantation house. Remmie was rubbing her hands over the smooth oak at the very moment Fanny ran to her after learning that Remmie's mother had been thrown from the horse carriage and killed. Fanny's normally steely exterior was overwhelmed as emotions ripped at her throat, leaving no room for sound to emerge. Although it was a few moments before the words finally surfaced, Remmie knew something was terribly wrong.

That was the day her mother died. That was *the* day, a day that was etched upon her young brain. Every day since when Remmie had walked past the newel cap, she was catapulted back to the horror of that day. Fanny could do little to help the child in her immense, pitch-black grief. It wasn't until late one night several months later, that Fanny removed the newel cap from the top of the post, snuck out into the night and threw it into the river.

The memory was as solid as the oak wood that the newel cap was made from. It had physical size and structure; it was something she could touch, and feel. The memory may as well have been made of oak as well because it was something that would not rot, wear, or break down, at least not in her lifetime. It would not release itself from her heart. Since the time her mother had died, the newel cap had symbolically sat in the center of her chest where it obstructed her heart.

Birds began leaping from her arms into the air. They fluttered in groups or two or three while feathers of vibrant red, green, and vermilion sprayed about the air in a torrent of wind currents. One bird hovered just in front of her and looked straight into the reflection of itself in her eyes. It was looking for the reflection of its own eye. It was looking for the twinkle-winkle.

Remmie felt warmth. And that warmth rode up her spine and settled her breathing. The bird then landed on her face with the softness of a butterfly. It stretched its red-plumed wings across her eyes and blocked her vision. The other birds still hovering plunged straight at her from all sides. They flew towards her torso and disappeared into its depths. Once inside, each bird gripped its talons into a corner of the newel cap and clamped down on it. Had it been made of flesh, the talons would have sunk in, but since the exterior of the oak was so hard, the talons only dented into the surface.

Remmie felt the rush of fluttering wings inside her, yet she did not alarm. She simply stood; arms extended, and basked in the knowledge that whatever they were doing, it was something wonderful.

The birds thrashed and struggled within her chest, and pulled with all their might against the newel cap. The cap was so tightly latched onto her heart that it had grown into the very muscle. As Remmie realized what they were doing, a well of emotion rose inside her. It started at her toes and etched its way up into her ankles. Once inside her feet, the emotions rushed up her legs like the surge of a volcano. When it reached her heart, it collided with force against the newel cap, pushing it loose. The cap wrenched free and the birds yanked it out of her chest and flew off into the distance. As the emotions released from her chest, they erupted upwards once again and rocked out of her in the form of tears.

As the bird on her face leapt off, Remmie felt as light as air and even looked down to see if she was floating. At that moment, the hundreds of other birds began to slowly decrease the volume of music they were playing. As the volume decreased, so did the tempo, until finally the music stopped.

Remmie surveyed the beautiful birds through the prisms of light formed from her tears. She wiped her eyes and found the birds looking at her and walking forward with heads held low. She sat and waited as they surrounded her, nuzzling her at all sides. Sounds gurgled out of their throats—something like the purr of a kitten, or the flutter of a dove. She held her hands low and others nuzzled their heads against her palms. She felt love like she'd never known. This was a place of peace, a place of love. This was the Magic Place.

In front of her, the birds parted, and formed a pathway between them. A litany of colorful feathers lay like confetti on top of the flower petals that lined the forest floor. The pathway widened until it was about five feet across. The volume of their purring increased as did their motion. They seemed to be lowering themselves to ground level, and then standing upright.

Remmie looked all around herself. Thousands of birds acted in unison and began hopping off the ground like popcorn. What they were becoming excited about, she did not know. As their volume began to reach the level of the cheering of a crowd, a blurry light appeared at the end of the forest path. The shape glowed about the edges, and white light shone from its center. As the figure walked forward, its long white gown wafted back and forth in the light breeze. The closer it got, the more it came into focus.

Remmie stared into the light coming from its chest. The light was the shape of a human heart, and was the purest white she'd ever seen. Remmie could not avert her eyes from the heart; it was beating rapidly and Remmie's eyes widened at the sight. The figure's long blond hair drifted both on and off its shoulders in a manner more consistent to being underwater. When it was around ten feet away, the faint breeze shifted, and blew towards Remmie. The strong aroma of jasmine hit her and the focus of the face sharpened—it was her mother.

20
The Magic Place

Jupiter became at once lost in his own world. He may as well have walked into the Magic Place alone, because he was now on his own, oblivious to Remmie calling after him. The boy ran down the path, not too fast at first, but more akin to the speed of a person afraid they might crash into someone around the next bend. It was the speed of excitement with just a jigger of apprehension.

He had no idea what lay ahead, but what he did know was that this was the most beautiful place he'd ever seen. And somewhere deep down inside, he knew nothing here would hurt him. Like a bloodhound at dinnertime, every so often Jupiter would stop, close his eyes, and smell deeply. As he suspected, the aroma was a mix between freshly split lighter wood and a fine supper of ham hocks, biscuits, gravy, chitlins, and cornbread—all cooking on an open fire. The boy lived in a perpetual state of hunger and he could only hope to be invited to such a feast.

Jupiter rounded back and forth as the path curved one way, then the next. The wisteria flower petals coating the path bounced and danced under his feet, some sticking to the worn leather soles of his tattered shoes. The smell of hickory smoke rose in his nostrils and he began to hear the telltale cracking of a campfire and the sizzle of pork fat on a cast iron skillet.

The smoke became visible, wafting its way in between branches of an enormous tree, and as Jupiter slowed his pace, bright orange light glowed in between its leaves. He quieted his steps, afraid he may be approaching a place he was not invited. But as he came around the last tree, he saw a man hunched over the campfire, tending to several pots of food splayed across the top of the glowing coals. The man was facing away from him, and appeared to be in full concentration over his work. Jupiter stopped and waited. As the man continued, he hummed in rhythm with the singing of the birds. To his right sat a small pile of lighter wood, each piece cut into a squared shaft, about a foot long, and the width of a pinky finger. After a moment, the man stopped. His head rose and he stood straight up. He was a tall man of African decent dressed in the tattered clothing of a slave. When he turned his head to the side, Jupiter immediately recognized him. It was his father, Washington.

"Daddy?" said the boy.

"Jupiter!"

The boy ran forward and hugged his father around the waist, looking up at him the way every boy looks to his hero.

"Daddy? Where are we? Me and Remmie, we found this path," the boy said, speaking with an auctioneer's speed, "in the woods and, and, we followed it, and it led us here. And, and..."

Washington laughed and held his son tight, "Whoa there my little man. Slow down, you're gonna use up all the words inside you before my ears can even suck them up."

"But what is the place, Daddy?" He was breathless.

Washington cocked his head upward and looked all about. "This here is a special place, indeed," he said. "In fact," he looked Jupiter in the eye, "this place is more than special. This here place is called the *Magic Place*." Jupiter reveled, clinging to every word as though they were goblets of food for him to consume. "Yessirree, this here is the Magic Place, and it's the only place on earth like it." He knelt down on one knee and sat the boy on his leg. "Now Jupiter, I want you to think about what I'm about to say."

"But Daddy!" interrupted the boy, "you gonna get in trouble, in trouble with the drivers! You've got to get back to work. They're gonna be mad..." Jupiter gasped in and out as he realized his father would be in danger.

"Slow down, now little man, slow down. There ain't no trouble in here. Nossirree, ain't no trouble in here at all. See, this place hasn't got anything bad in it. Ain't got no darkness, nor slavery, nor hunger, nor pain, nor sadness. This here is the Magic Place." He canted his head to the side and held the boy by the face. "Jupiter, this place, is a little slice of heaven brought down to earth."

"I believe it!" said the boy, relieved his father would not be punished for being absent from work.

But Washington knew the boy had not comprehended what it would mean for them to be standing *in* heaven. "Little man," he said with a serious tone, "Jesus put this little piece of heaven on earth for his own reasons, and I think I know why he led you down that path."

"Why?"

"He wanted you to see me."

"But Daddy! I get to see you every night!" But then a thought struck Jupiter with the force of an anvil—*what if that means Daddy is in heaven?* "But Daddy, if Jesus led me and Remmie down that path, why...why are you here?" Before the question had left his mouth, he already knew the answer—the thought slammed into his head. *Daddy is dead, Daddy is dead.* Jupiter leaned his head into Washington's chest and screamed, "You ain't dead! No, you ain't!" Even though his father had proclaimed that in this place there was no sadness, tears began a steady trickle, then worked up to a stream, and finally into a river's torrent.

Though the wailing was unbearable, Washington said nothing. He held his son with love, and caressed his head. After several minutes, the sobs subsided.

"You can't be dead, Daddy, you can't. Who's gonna take care of me? Who's gonna help me get something to eat and tell me bedtime stories and, and..."

"Shhhh, little man, it's all gonna be okay. You're gonna miss me, just as sure as you're born, you are. But you are gonna be just fine. Fanny is gonna watch over you like you was one of her own young-uns, she is."

Jupiter wiped tears from his face, "I thought you said there wasn't any sadness here."

"You right, yessirree. I did say that. But see, it goes like this— there's no sadness here *for everybody that lives here.* And you, well, you're just visiting."

"You mean I don't live here with you?"

"No, little man, you don't. Not yet anyways. See, my time has come, and I'm gonna spend e-ternity in heaven. And I tell you a secret, this is the best place you've ever thought of. But you've got more time before you come. You've got work to do, yessirree, you do. But even though you still have things to do on earth, Jesus wanted you to come in here for a reason. You, and Remmie too. I'm not sure what all his reason's are; he didn't exactly say. But when you feel it on the inside, you'll know. Yessirree you'll know. But, I've got me a feeling he's gonna give you some kind of gift."

"You mean like maybe some good shoes, and clothes, and maybe some books, so I can learn my reading, writing, and 'rithmatic? Oh that'd be grand Daddy, that'd be so grand." Jupiter's smile widened.

"Oh," laughed Washington, "I don't think it will be a gift like those, no, no. I think, it'll be a gift bigger'n all them put together. But you just wait, yessirree, you just wait and see."

21
Something Unexpected

Mr. Winkles and the children had followed Remmie and Jupiter down the path that led to the poison ivy tree, watched them disappear, and followed behind them into the Magic Place where they witnessed the things that had happened to them both.

"Hey, Mr. Winkles?" said Lenny. "You know, Jupiter's daddy says that same thing as you."

"And what's that, little man?"

"And hey! That's another!" the boy continued. "Jupiter's daddy always says *yessirree* and *sure as you're born*, and he also calls Jupiter *little man*. You always say those things too. How come you always say those same things?"

Winkles was almost heard to mumble, "Sometimes a son imitates his father," but no one noticed. "Well," he said, "now I know you children got lots of questions, yessirree. So let's get to it!"

Lenny's confidence brimmed and he continued his control of the conversation. "So, what is this Magic Place? Is it really heaven?"

"It sure is, it surely is. It is heaven on earth. It's just a little slice of heaven, brought right down here to earth, yessirree."

The little girl stepped up in quick succession, "So, that whole path, that whole path we walked down, it's just there to lead people to heaven? Back home, can I just go find a path out in the woods that leads to heaven? Is that how folks get there?"

"Oh my. Oh, well, see, this is a special path. And no, ain't no path we could get on today out in the woods near school that's like this one. Nossirree. This is a special path indeeeed."

"Mr. Winkles," said Lenny, tugging on his sweater, "something's bothering me. How come Jupiter can't smell the jasmine, and Remmie can't smell the...what was it?"

"Lighter wood. Fresh cut lighter wood."

"What is lighter wood anyway? How come they can't smell what each other are smelling? It doesn't make any sense."

Winkles smiled at the boy. "You've brought up an interesting thing, little man. Yessirree, just as sure as you're born, you done. Lighter wood comes from an old pine tree. The tree dies, and all the sap inside seeps down towards the base. That sap makes the wood all hard and such. And, when you split it, it not only smells wonderful, but it's so good for helping you start a campfire because it burns so well. Anyway, here in the Magic Place, things aren't like they are in regular places. This is a piece of heaven on earth, so things act like they do in heaven. In heaven, everybody has kind of got their own heaven. They see things not everybody else can see. They smell things not everybody else can smell. Things might look a whole lot different from one person to the next." He surveyed the faces, "That make sense?"

"So, you mean, heaven might be different for me than for you?"

"That's right. See, heaven is *your* perfect place, just for you. Now, that doesn't mean you won't be spending time with all the other folks in heaven, and having fun and visiting and spending time with your kinfolk. But y'all might be experiencing things differently, depending on what your perfect heaven is."

"So Jupiter knows that his daddy died?"

"Yes, honey, he does. And notice how Jupiter's all sad about it? Well, like his daddy told him, there's no sadness in heaven. But since Jupiter isn't really living in heaven just yet, he's gonna feel that sadness."

"But what about the presents?" said the pigtails.

Mr. Winkles cocked his head to the side. "Presents? What do you mean, honey?"

"They're supposed to get presents. Like Jupiter's daddy said. He said Jupiter would be getting a present."

"Oh!" laughed Winkles, "you mean a *gift*, a gift. Oh my, yessirree. Well, what he's talking about is a gift from God himself.

See, God's gonna give Jupiter a special gift. The gift is that Jupiter, when he leaves here, will be able to bring folks back into the Magic Place. Yessirree, he's the only one that can do it, too! Oh, it's such a special gift. Just imagine, being able to bring folks in to *heaven* on earth!"

Several sets of eyes went wide. Lenny in particular, shook his head up and down, obviously pleased with the gift.

"You like that gift, don't you?"

"You bet I do," said Lenny. "That's a great gift. If I'd had a gift like that, I could have brought my daddy in there, and I would have made him go..." The thought played forward in his head, and he saddened.

Winkles ruffled his fingers through Lenny's hair. "Just as sure as as you're born, you could," he said, "yessirree."

"He can bring anybody?" whispered Lenny above his tightened throat. "Hey, wait a minute. But it was you that led us into the Magic Place. I thought you said Jupiter was the only one that could do that."

But Mr. Winkles blew past the observation.

"And y'all have got to understand something. Not just *any*-body can get in to heaven, but almost." He rubbed his unshaven chin, and considered how to best explain. "Not everybody that dies, goes to heaven, do they? Some folks never believed, did they? They never believed in God, or Jesus, nor nuthin'. And, their heart is all filled...you know, filled with that ugly color of rotten pumpkin? Y'all know what I'm talking about? Dark orange and black and stuff?" His tone dropped an octave. "That means their heart is covered in *wickedness*, and it fills up with the dirt of sin. But even folks whose heart is full of sin can get into heaven, if they ask."

"You mean, you can just ask and get into heaven?" said Lenny with more than a touch of incredulousness. "Who do I ask about getting into heaven. Do I ask my momma?"

"No," cackled Mr. Winkles, "but, you do ask Jesus. Jesus *is* God, and he loves all of us, even the wicked ones. Folks just have to ask Jesus to come into their heart. And if that happens, well..."

The little girl covered her eyes and low, but distinct whimpers fluttered out.

"Well little Missy, what's the matter now darlin'? Hold on now. Mr. Winkles has just one rule, and that is that nobody is allowed to cry alone in his presence, heh-heh. So come on up here, little one. You get up in my arms here. Tell Mr. Winkles what's wrong."

"I can't," she blubbered.

"Well sure you can."

"I can't tell. I can't tell no one."

"But you can always tell Mr. Winkles. Haven't we been through a lot together today? Now come on, tell Mr. Winkles what's the matter."

She exploded, "I can't ask Jesus to come into my heart!" She burst into tears and buried her head onto his neck. Her sobs blubbered, but in one burst, she said, "I can't ask Jesus into my heart! It's all dirty in there! I can't, I can't, I can't!" A tiny tear etched the dusty fabric of his sweater.

He held her in tight. "Shhh, shhh. It's gonna be okay. You'll be seein'. It's gonna be just fine."

They rocked back and forth as the girl settled down. Mr. Winkles eyes glistened as he fought back emotions of his own. "Now, I want to tell all of you something, and I want to hear me, and hear me good." Every eye locked on him. "There's no such thing as a heart that has too much dirt in it for Jesus. Ain't no heart that has too much dirt in it. It's not possible. Y'all all understand old Mr. Winkles?"

He surveyed their faces, looking to each one, ensuring every pair of eyes registered back against his.

"And you, little Missy, you understand?"

She nodded her head in ascent.

"Well, okay then. So, where were we?"

Lenny grabbed Mr. Winkles by the arm, "But what about my friend Shimon? What about Shimon?"

Winkles looked down at the other children. "Sounds like something important Lenny's got to say, now doesn't it?" He turned back to Lenny. "Well, what about your friend Shimon?"

"You said to get to heaven you have to ask Jesus into your heart."

"I did say that."

"My friend Shimon...his family is Jewish, and they don't believe in Jesus, do they?"

Mr. Winkles stood up tall again. "For such a little man, you sure do bring some big questions. So, let's talk about that thing there. Y'all all gather around, and sit criss-cross applesauce." Once the children were seated, he began. "Good! See, not all folks believe in Jesus, no they don't, nossirree. And guess what?" he leaned forward, "Lots of folks don't think about it, but Jesus himself was a Jew."

The children looked across at each other, but not a sound was heard until Lenny piped up.

"I thought he was a Christian."

"Well, Jesus was *the Christ*. A Christian is someone who follows the Christ. So, he didn't exactly follow himself. Instead, he was a Jew and the folks that followed him were, and are, Christians. And you know what else? Since Jesus was born all the way over in Israel, you know what? He doesn't look like a white man either."

Several of the children's eyes widened.

"No he doesn't. Think about that. The folks born in Israel have darker skin than most white folks, don't they? And they most times have hair as black as mine. Well, maybe as black as mine was, before it turned gray!" The children laughed. "Anyway, you have to know lots about Jesus to understand him. But, don't worry. Jesus doesn't think bad of you just because you think about him looking like a white man. Everybody thinks about the way Jesus looks in his own way, and he doesn't mind none. But anyway, like I was saying, Jesus was a Jewish man, and the folks that all believed in him, believed he was what we call, The Christ. That means he was the son of God himself. So, since the followers believed he was The Christ, they become known as *Christians*—the ones that followed The Christ. But even though Jesus was The Christ, that doesn't mean he wasn't still a Jew, now does it?" He laid out the words as one stating fact.

"But if Shimon doesn't believe in Jesus! Mr. Winkles, he can't, he can't," the boy spoke faster; "he can't go to heaven!"

Winkles held up both hands, palms out, to Lenny. "Hold on there, little man. Just hold those horses. We're still getting to that part. Mr. Winkles is gonna ex-plain. So, let's talk about this here thing with our friends the Jews. A long, long time ago, way before you were born, and even way before Jesus was born, God had chosen his people. And out of all the folks in the whole world, he chose the Jews. Way, way back then, the Jews were rebelling and not worshiping God, and they were even worshiping something else." He looked up into the trees as if he might pluck a word out of the air. "They were worshiping something called Baal. Kind of sounds like a bale of hay, doesn't it? So God got mad at them for worshiping something else, and so he did something the bible calls *hardening their hearts*. It means that since they already made up their minds about worshiping this Baal, he made it so they couldn't change their minds about it. After that, God did something, well, it isn't purty, but God made sure most of those folks eventually died." The children looked dismayed. "But, he saved seven thousand of them. Seven thousand! Yessirree. He saved a whole mess of them, didn't he?"

"Yeah, but how did he know who to save?" said Lenny.

Winkles looked down, "I'm gonna tell you how God knew who he was gonna save, and that's the bestest part. God saved seven thousand Jewish folks that were the ones who were worshiping *him*, and not that old Baal-o-hay. Ain't that a story?"

A few of the children whispered back and forth.

"Now y'all listen here. There's one thing Mr. Winkles wants you children to remember about all this." Winkles wagged his finger, "The reason God saved them folks, was because they believed in *him*. Not believed in Jesus, because Jesus hadn't come yet, but believed in him, the father. Do you all know what that means? That means he saved them by grace, and not because of something nice they did, nor because they were helping other folks out, or none of that. They got saved and they are gonna go to heaven, because of what they *believed*."

He looked over at Lenny, and put his hand on the boy's shoulder.

"Lenny, your friend Shimon, he's gonna go to heaven too, yessirree. See, God hasn't forgotten his chosen folks, and he's not finished with them either. So now, let's talk about the time, way after God chose the seven thousand, when Jesus was walking the earth. So, when Jesus was walking the earth, there were Jews all around him." He swung his arms in a wide arc, "And some of them decided they believed in him, and some of them didn't. Kind of sounds just like before he chose the seven thousand, don't it?" Fire and excitement welled up from his gut, "Them ones that believed became *Christians*," the word tasted like ice cream on a hot summer day. "But that doesn't mean they're not still Jews too. Y'all don't look so confused. And Lenny, you pay attention too, because this is about your friend, Shimon. It just means that if your grand-mamma was a Jew, and your daddy was a Jew, and everybody in your family was a Jew, you ain't got to leave all of that behind you to be a Christian."

"I don't get it," said Lenny, in a matter-of-fact tone.

"It's just like the way the Jews were who were around Jesus. They were Jews, right? But when they came to believe he was God's only-est son, they added their new belief in the son to their old belief in the father. Anyhow, for the others around Jesus that *didn't* believe, well, you might think God was madder than a farmer looking at a whole crop full of boll weevils, yessirree. But, he wasn't. Y'all got to understand," he was up on his feet nearly dancing, "God's got a way of making sure we all experience being on the *outside*, so he can open the door for us himself, and welcome us all back to the *inside*."

The pigtails perked out of her silence, "So, you mean God wasn't real mad at those folks for not believing?"

"Oh, no, he wasn't exactly *thrilled* about the whole thing," he laughed. "But what it mean is, some day, he's gonna convince all his chosen people to believe in Jesus, yessirree. It's written down in the good book that once Jesus comes back again, all his chosen people are gonna be made right with God. No, he ain't mad at them, he loves his chosen folk."

Mr. Winkles waited until he was sure they all understood.

After several moments of silence, his brow went up. "Who wants know about Remmie?"

Hands rose all over, and several voices blurted all at the same time, "Oooh, me! I do, I do."

The pigtails' voice overpowered the rest, "Yeah, what about Remmie? Does she get a present too? Kind of like Jupiter? Does she get a present? Is it like Christmas morning?"

"Lots of questions, lllllllots of questions," laughed Winkles. "Yes, little Missy. She gets a present. See children, everybody that finds their way into the Magic Place comes out with a *special* gift. And that gift is meant just for them. But, truth be told, ain't many folks been into the Magic Place and then back out again. There have been a few, but not many. Y'all see? And there's something else y'all have got to know, because y'all already have some gifts of your own." He cupped his hand to his mouth and whispered, "A gift from God himself is something he's meaning you to use."

"You already told us that," quipped Lenny.

"Well, what does she get? What does she get?" The little girl's pigtails bounced up and down.

Mr. Winkles paid her no mind, but instead looked at them as a group. "Y'all know, even though there haven't been many folks that have come back out of the Magic Place, the ones that have, I've seen the gifts they got! I've seen all kinds of wonderful gifts. And the one Remmie got is soooo, so special. It's special to her, but in our story today she doesn't yet know why." He leaned down towards their little faces, "Remmie got the gift of what I call, *The Seeing*."

"What's The Seeing, Mr. Winkles?" asked the pigtails. Jitters ran across her like she had consumed a triple espresso.

He spoke as though revealing a prophecy, "The Seeing is a gift where Remmie is now able to look at a person, and see their heart."

"Hey," said Lenny. "You told us you had a friend that had gotten that gift. Are you trying to trick us or something? You said your friend could see The Shining colors, right? Is Remmie your friend? Wait, she can't be, this story happened a long time ago."

Winkles cleared his throat; an obvious attempt to avoid the question.

The pigtails flopped up and down, "She can see a person's heart?" Then a fresh coating of confusion slopped across her face, and she stopped bouncing.

"Oh," said Winkles, "she can do more than just look inside, and see your heart beating, yessirree." He held his hand in the shape of a ball and stared at it as he described the full extent of the gift. "Once Remmie realizes what she's been given, she's gonna be able to look at a person, and see clear down to they're soul." He continued as though he was telling a ghost tale. "She can see what lay upon their heart, what's bothering them, and what kind of worries they have." He stood tall and the children's eyes followed his. "She's also gonna see the color of their heart."

"The color? Oooo, but isn't it kind of bloody and stuff?" said the little girl.

"Well, not like that kind of color, little Missy. No, see, a person's heart has a special kind of color to it. Depending on the color, it tells if they are sad, or if they're happy. And...some much more important stuff too."

"Like what, Mr. Winkles?"

"Well, if you've got the gift of The Seeing, you can see if their heart is full of righteousness or of wickedness, like I talked about earlier. That make sense, little Missy?"

"I dunno." Her face crinkled and she put her finger to her mouth. "What's righ-chussss-ness?"

"Righteousness! It's kind of like goodness, or maybe kind of like when a person is honorable. You know, they're always trying to do the right thing? See, being good means you feel the love of Christ. It's not that being Christian means you are good, instead it means that bringing God in your heart makes you feel like you want to do good things." He looked at her with dissatisfaction, "Hmmm, you know Missy, that space on your head in between those pigtails looks like it still has some questions."

She put her hands on her hips—it was the best impersonation she could do of her mother. "Goodness has a color?" The disbelief was evident.

"Oh yes!" he exclaimed, then knelt down onto one knee. "Oh children, goodness has a beautiful color." His hands waved across the sky. "It's kind of hard to describe, but it looks a lot like the glow of yellow at sunrise. Y'all know that yellow? But, it's got more than just that one color. It's also got that special something that you see at sunrise. When the golden yellow is coming up all around, and it has a *shine* to it." His eyes went as wide as his smile, and he sounded off like a preacher, "It's got a *glory* to it. Yessirree! If you have the gift of The Seeing, you can't mistake seeing that color in somebody's heart."

"Well, what's she gonna do with a gift like that?" said Lenny. "I mean, how come she didn't get the gift of knowing the future, or turning rocks into gold or something fun?"

"Lenny, some gifts are things we don't always understand, at first. But, we're gonna see what Remmie does with her gift. Yep, just as sure as you're born, we gonna. And something else. God gives us a gift for a reason. But, it's one of *his* reasons, not one of your reasons. Okay?"

The boy studied the tops of his Converse high tops. "Okay, Mr. Winkles," he said as he shifted some pine straw to the side.

"You're a good boy. I bet if Remmie was right here, she'd look at you, and she'd say you've got a good heart, Lenny. A good heart." He looked over at the little pigtails, "And she would say you've got a good heart too, little Missy. And all of y'all."

Little Missy looked at him with puppy-dog eyes.

The old man continued, "And you know something else? Lots of times, Jesus doesn't work the way we expect him to, does he? Nossirree, he doesn't. I'm just thinking, do you all remember when Remmie and Jupiter first started down this trail that led them to the Magic Place? Who remembers?"

Every hand shot into the air.

"That's good, that's good. It means y'all have been paying attention." But he knew the children had hung on his every word. It was as if each word was a glass of water in the middle of a parched desert. "Who remembers what marked the very start of the trail?"

The children looked back and forth at one another, until at last, Lenny let his hand move up, just a bit at first, then it climbed slow but steady.

"What was it, little man?"

"The thing that marked the top of the trail was that thing that held still."

Mr. Winkles eyes crinkled, then he looked far left, then right, his confusion apparent. "Something that held still? Oh! You're right! But it wasn't something that *held* still, it was that thing that is *called* a still. Hmmm, y'all still ain't too sure about what a still is, are you? Well, that's okay. I wanna talk about it some more, so y'all see if you can remember it."

He leaned towards them again.

"A still is something that men use to make moonshine. And moonshine is something that men drink, and it's as strong as an ox pulling a plow, yessirree!" He spoke out of the side of his mouth, "Moonshine is what gets a man drunk. Y'all know what drunk is?" With all the heads nodding, he knew they were now tracking. "So, a still was sitting right there, tall and proud, right smack dab at the top of the trail leading to the Magic Place. And y'all remember what the Magic Place is—it's heaven, right here on earth, ain't it? So, I ask you, what is a moonshine-making still doing as the marker to the beginning of the trail leading to heaven?"

Not even Lenny's hand budged.

"Well let old Mr. Winkles tell y'all. Y'all remember what I was just saying about how sometimes Jesus does things that ain't exactly expected? Well, that's because Jesus *himself* ain't exactly what was expected."

"Mr. Winkles?" said the pigtails as she pulled against his sweater. "I don't understand any of that. What happened? Did Jesus come over for supper without anyone knowing he was coming?"

Winkles roared back in laughter, "Oh, little Missy, that's a good one! Jesus coming over to supper!" He settled down and wiped his brow. "No, he didn't come over to supper without being invited. No, what I means is, the folks way back in the day, back two thousand years ago, were expecting something else entirely. They were thinking that when the Christ came, that he'd be somebody that would take over the whole place, and take all the Jewish folks, and be their king. But Jesus wasn't like that, was he? No, he wasn't. He didn't act like a king. Not like an earthly king, anyway. Instead, he was always going around healing folks that were sick, and helping them, and turning water into wine, and making a blind man see and stuff like that. Yet that's how he was. Those folks weren't expecting anybody like that, and that is why lots of them just didn't believe he was the son of God. And it didn't matter that some of them were right beside him when he was performing a miracle."

Lenny piped up. "Was Jesus making moonshine, Mr. Winkles?"

Winkles laughed again, "No, no Lenny. He wasn't making moonshine. But, he did make that water into wine though. So, you're asking about the still, right? See, I think that old still is sitting at the top of that trail just to remind us that sometimes things aren't going to be like we expect. Nobody would have thought that God would choose a young, unmarried girl to give birth to Jesus, and nobody would be thinking that a still, used by bad men to make moonshine, would be marking a trail leading to heaven."

He paused, and looked to each child.

"Y'all know what I'm thinking? I think he's telling us that whatever Remmie does with her gift," the next words trailed off his tongue with the flutter of a duck's wings, "it might just be something we wouldn't expect."

22
A Vision of Lights

Jupiter woke with a start. His heart jumped, but once he saw Remmie beside him, he calmed.

"Remmie, Remmie. Wake up. Wake up girl."

Her eyes opened and her face plastered with confusion.

"That place, that place is like magic. But what are we doing out here in the woods?" said Jupiter. "I don't even remember leaving that Magic Place."

Remmie's mouth hung open, her eyes dotted with sleep. "I don't remember leaving either." She rubbed her eyes and then looked off over her shoulder. "But there's the still over there, so we haven't gone far. How long have we been here?"

The two stood in trepidation, each looking far and wide through the trees to see if anyone was watching. The only sound came from the wings of a barred owl that was likely searching for an early lunch, or perhaps, a springtime mate. The owl landed on the dead branch of a nearby pine, then heaved out its telltale call, "*Whoop, whoop, wha, woooo. Whoop, whoop, wha, woooo.*" They stared after it, but when the call wasn't returned by another owl the plump bird leapt off the branch and continued its daily ritual.

"Remmie?" said Jupiter. "Remmie, something terrible happened, something terrible."

"What are you talking about? We just came out of the most amazing place God ever put here." But the boy's eyes spoke of his sorrow.

"My daddy..." he whimpered. "He's gone now." Jupiter's lip puckered and stifled sobs ushered out.

"Jupiter? What are you talking about?"

"I saw my daddy. I saw him. He was in there, back in there, in that Magic Place."

"No, no, it can't be. That place," she looked off through the trees and pictured the golden bricks at the entrance, "that place is more than magic. It's a little piece of heaven, right here on earth. I know it is, I saw my momma."

"That's what I'm telling you. I saw my daddy. He said there was an accident and he died, and he's in heaven now. He died, Remmie, he died." The torrential loss engulfed the child.

"He was...oh, oh, Jupiter! Oh, Jupiter, I'm so sorry. I'm so sorry," and she clasped her mouth in a fruitless effort to contain the sadness. The emotions whirled inside her—the loss of Jupiter's father, having just seen her own mother, and the feelings of loss that that dredged up.

Not only was she sad for Jupiter's loss, but looking directly at him was difficult. Something glowed in Remmie's vision. To her, it seemed that there was something stuck in her eye, and she could not blink it out. She closed her eyes and held Jupiter tight. They stayed there for what might have been several minutes. When they separated, she again had trouble with her vision. Remmie crunched her eyes shut and rubbed them, but each time they reopened, the same odd light glowed. The glowing was coming from Jupiter's chest.

"What's the matter Remmie? You keep rubbing your eyes. Something wrong?"

Remmie held them shut and continued the useless rubbing. "My eyes, there must be something stuck in them. I can't get it free."

"Do they hurt?"

She opened her eyes, but this time looked at the metallic still that sat not twenty feet away. Her vision had returned to normal. She next looked off into the trees, and finally, over into a thicket of palmettos—the glow she had seen a moment before was now gone. But when she looked back at Jupiter, she screamed. There, in the center of his chest, a bright white light glowed.

"Remmie!" panicked Jupiter, "Remmie! What's wrong!? What's wrong?" He made frantic efforts to hold her by the shoulders, but she thrashed back and forth against the disturbing visions.

"I can't, I can't," she yelled, "my eyes...I don't understand..."

"Remmie, you're scaring me! What's wrong?"

She shook herself free from his grasp, then opened her eyes one more time. "Jupiter," she said, "when I look at you, there's...there's something wrong. It looks like something is glowing inside of you, right up here."

Jupiter looked down at his tattered overalls, half expecting it to be true, but could see nothing.

"It's there," she said. "It is. I'm looking right at it. It's bright, a bright white light. I don't know what it is."

"I don't see nuthin'."

But no sooner had he spoken did they both hear a sound approaching in the distance. They froze, still very unsure of what was happening. The sound grew louder and became distinguishable as heavy footsteps—someone was running. Both children crouched to the ground. Moments later, the footsteps stopped with abruptness. Both remained motionless, fearing even the act of breathing might give away their position.

"Jupiter!" yelled a voice, "Jupiter!" It was the fourteen-year-old slave boy, gasping to catch his breath.

23
A Brackish Ending

Mordecai's fear welled until his gut burned. He'd only known one other slave driver that had been held responsible in the death of a slave, and that man had been run out of the county and narrowly escaped a beating. The only way to avoid it would be to pay the plantation owner the fair market price for the loss of his property, and there was no way Mordecai could pay such a sum.

With the constant pangs in his stomach, Mordecai's bad temper went into overdrive. It was like the hair-trigger on a rifle—just a breath could set it off. And the worst part was the waiting. Graydon Moon hadn't emerged from the plantation house all day, and it was now towards evening. *What could he be thinking?* And, more importantly, *why had the master's horse-drawn carriage ridden away in such haste not an hour after the accident?* Surely Graydon Moon had sent word to town of the entire affair. Would the Sheriff be summoned to arrest Mordecai for the destruction of property, property that he could not repay? Would a mob arrive later that night? Mordecai shivered, it was his simple mind's only defense.

What he must concentrate on now were the last orders given to him. Graydon Moon's voice echoed in his head—*the field must be planted and flooded by morning.* Washington's dead body was still pinned beneath the stump. And with no sign of being able to free it, Mordecai was left with only one choice—to move forward based on the last known orders from Graydon Moon. Despite the vocal grieving of the slaves, he had ordered the planting of rice seeds to begin earlier in the day. And that work continued to this hour.

The wailing cries at the loss of Washington, the head of their clan, would not stop. The sounds began ingraining themselves into Mordecai's mind, filling it with what felt like little shards of glass that floated to the far corners of his head. *But the planting must continue*, he thought. The worst of it was that the gates that now held firm against the brackish river tides must be opened. The rice field would be flooded with Washington's body still resting within, pinned underneath the stump.

24
The Voice of the Witch

Remmie and Jupiter crouched low in fear of being discovered so near to the still. Neither one breathed, and they stared into the palmetto thicket, in the direction of the voice. They were unable to see any further than the length of a horse, and dared not stand up.

"Juuuuuuu-pit-errrrr," yelled the youthful voice.

Jupiter grabbed Remmie by the shoulder and crouched into her, "It's the ghost!" his broken voice whispered. "Remmie, it's the ghost of that witch. She's come for me!"

Remmie pushed him back and looked him in the eye. Her face washed clean of the fear that had earlier pained it, and she stood straight up. Jupiter pulled down against her, but she called out, "Over here. We're over here."

"What are you doing?" hampered Jupiter. "That witch..."

But she cut him off. "There is no witch. I told you already. And besides, it's not even a woman's voice. It's a man, or well, a boy's voice, anyway. Don't you recognize it? You big fraidey-cat."

"Miss Remmie? Where is you?" yelled back the teenager.

"Oh. Well, sure, I know it was that boy the whole time," said Jupiter.

"Uh, huh."

The teen had a stick-thin frame, and walked forward until he was in between them and the still. "Where y'all been? I been looking and looking."

Remmie noticed the boy was out of breath.

"What's the matter? You look like you've been running." "I has," he panted, "I has. It's, it's...they's something terrible happened. Something terrible."

Remmie knew what it was and so did Jupiter, but it was Jupiter that spoke first. "I know about it, I know."

"What you mean you know?"

"It's my daddy, ain't it? My daddy died, didn't he?" The knowledge of the event did nothing to ease the choking feeling in Jupiter's throat.

"How do you...? I don't understand."

"It's a long story, but, I know." A tear rolled off Jupiter's cheek, hurtled towards the ground, and shattered on the top of his bare foot.

"You seen it? You seen it happen?"

"No," said Jupiter, "I didn't see him get...no, but I saw my daddy though. I saw him in heaven. He told me what happened, and that he's gonna go up and live in heaven now." He cried as the last words spit out of his mouth.

"You done saw yo daddy in heaven? How you done that?"

Remmie spoke, her voice clear and driven. "I don't think it's something we can tell you. I think it's something we have to show you. But, not right now. Jupiter, we should get back. They're going to wonder where we've been."

25
Black Redness

When they got back to the rice field, the scene was awful. Jupiter averted his eyes to prevent looking in the direction of his father's body, which remained pinned under the massive stump. From his vantage point, the only thing he could see was his father's empty right shoe, which was stuck in the mud just outside the stump. It must have come off when Washington leapt into the pit to knock Leander clear.

The sight of it was enough. Jupiter already knew his father was gone, but he didn't want to see any more. As he turned his back to the muddy rice field, Fanny, the house slave, sat down beside him.

"I know, honey, I know. You just sit here a while with Fanny. Fanny's gonna take care of you now, yes she is. She gonna take care of you. And, you gonna live in the mastah's plantation house too."

Remmie stared out at the great stump. She squinted against the bright light pouring from the chests of the men who were fighting to pull it free. Her mind still had a hard time processing what she was seeing. Of the two dozen or more slaves, each man's chest glowed brightly. It was the same brilliant white light she'd seen inside Jupiter's chest. And, it was almost the same brilliant white light she'd seen glowing inside her mother as well. Her mind raced as she tried to comprehend the visions.

It wasn't until she saw a redness glowing behind the stump that her eyes finally focused. It was coming from Mordecai. From behind the stump he stepped and Remmie could see that his chest didn't glow with the white purity of new-fallen snow. Instead, it glowed with a black redness. And at that moment, Remmie knew what the visions meant. The white glow of a heart represented pure righteousness and belief in God, and the blackish red glow signified wickedness; thick, unadulterated evil.

The more she stared at the grouping of men, the clearer the colors became. As her mind adjusted to the sights, she started to notice that each slave's pure white, wasn't quite as pure and clean as she initially perceived. Each man's heart was mostly white, but slight shades of green, dappled specks of tan, and hues of pink competed with one another for space. It was like looking into a calabash, the gourd of a pumpkin used by slaves as a cooking pot, full of live crayfish, fighting with one another.

Her head nodded as she looked at each man in turn. Although each heart had elements of wickedness, the pure righteousness overpowered. She thought of her mother and the stunning radiance of her heart, and smiled. Remmie was unaware of the fact that Fanny had been talking to her the whole time.

"...Child? Child? Miss Remmie? Child, you okay?"

As Fanny reached out and touched her shoulder, Remmie startled.

"Oh! What? What?"

"You look like you was in a trace...child. You look white as a ghost." Fanny was a favorite of Remmie's. The woman had practically raised her after her mother died.

"What Fanny? No, no, I'm fine."

Fanny reworked her turban back onto her dirty hair. "Here, you sit yourself down, Miss Remmie. You don't look so well. You sit down right here next to good old Fanny."

26
Reasons

Mr. Winkles' class of children traversed back to the plantation house and stood in the thick bushes adorning the porch, watching the scene again at the rice field.

"Y'all stay crouched down behind these here bushes," whispered Winkles. "Shhhh," he said, holding a finger to his lips, "y'all stay real quiet so we can hear them and nobody sees us."

Lenny tugged at his sweater a little too hard, his boldness getting the best of him. "Oh, I'm sorry, Mr. Winkles."

"That's okay, Lenny. It's an old sweater. But let's stay quiet, so nobody hears us."

"That's what I was going to ask you about," continued his stern little face. "Can anybody really see us?"

Mr. Winkles' face met Lenny's. "Now what makes you ask that, Meestah Lenny?"

"I dunno. But it seems like one minute, we're all sitting under the oak trees outside the library, and the next minute, we're back on a slave plantation in the old South. Are we really here? Can any of these people really see us?"

Winkles considered this for a moment.

"Lenny," he started, "not everything is something we know the answers to. Know what I mean?" The boy had no reaction. "Sometimes, God just wants us to experience something. And lots of times, we don't know the *reasons* for it, or how it works. Okay?"

The boy was not entirely satisfied, but decided the question must have gone to the place where adults let questions die.

27
The Heart of Graydon

Fanny sat with the two children on the dike; their backs turned away from the rice field.

"Y'all both listen to old Fanny. Fanny gonna take care of both of y'all. You hear me? Jupiter, I'd do anything to bring your daddy back, but I can't. And Remmie, same for you. I'd do anything to bring your momma back. My momma always said, 'Can't worry none about what you can't control. Just worry about what you *can*.'" Her emphasis on the last word sunk into them.

Mr. Winkles pointed to the trio sitting on the dike.

"Did everybody hear that?" he said with a bit of emotion. "Y'all think about what Fanny did just then. She told them she's gonna be their momma. Now, she may be just a house slave, but God doesn't care anything about that. He don't care where you are, and what you're doing when he calls you for something important."

"Mr. Winkles?" whispered the pigtails.

"Yes, sweet pea?"

"Are you okay? You don't want us to see it, but you're crying. I don't want you to cry, Mr. Winkles. Please don't cry." The sudden show of emotion from the old man took the children by surprise.

"Thank you, little Missy."

"Why are you sad, Mr. Winkles?"

He stared off towards Fanny. "Sometimes," he could not continue at first. "Sometimes there are things folks say to us in our lives...sometimes it's something you never forget."

He rubbed her head. And although she did not understand what he meant, Lenny looked at him, then back at Fanny. He had added another piece to the puzzle that had been assembling in his mind. He was beginning to piece together who Mr. Winkles actually was.

"Mr. Winkles, there's something I've been wondering about. Remmie can see the hearts of those men and sometimes there's black in there. How does it get in there; into your heart, I mean?"

"How does it get into your heart? Well, that's a good-un, Meestah Lenny, a good-un. See, when we get separated from God, we let evil inside of us. That's the blackness. But evil can only be around when there isn't any goodness in there, see? It's kind of like the light and the dark. If there's no light around, everything's all dark. It's things like pain, holding a grudge against somebody, wickedness, not showing love to others, and stuff like that that separates us from God in the first place. If we let the love of God in our heart, all the dark goes away. Heck, that's God's whole purpose—to turn darkness into light."

In the backdrop of the rice field, men strained and pulled against the ropes wrapped around the stump. Jupiter could see a fight in their eyes. The fervency of their desire to free his father's body was evident in their furled brows. Mordecai tossed his hands into the air and yelled for them to stop. It was no use. The stump would not budge. The slave driver that they despised most was now to tell them to leave the body of their lost friend.

"Y'all stop now. Ain't no use; it ain't gonna work. We can't waist no more time on this. A'sides, he's gone anyway. No use losing another day."

The men did not budge, but stared Mordecai into a pause.

"I said we're done!" he yelled, taking off his hat and flailing it at them. "Get off of here! We're floodin' this here field!"

From the bank, Remmie stood up. "But...you can't flood the field. Poor Jupiter's daddy is still out there."

Fanny pulled against her, but she yanked free. "No! No! It can't be allowed." She turned towards the plantation house and ran, "Father!" she screamed. "Fatherrrrrrrrr!"

Fanny was up now, "Child, don't. Child, Fanny's here. Fanny gonna make it all right."

But Remmie would have none of it, and continued running towards the porch. By the time she leapt the steps, her father had emerged. The two nearly collided.

"What incarnation?" said Graydon Moon.

"Father! Father, don't let them do it. That evil Mordecai is going to flood the field!"

"Calm down, Remmie. My goodness. You'd think a hurricane was about to come upon us the way you're carrying on."

The statement seemed to take meaning as a strong gust of wind picked up, seemingly out of nowhere. In the rice field, Mordecai recapped his hat and held it in place against the hot wind. Even Remmie turned to look in its direction. But, she would not be dissuaded.

"Father! You can't let him! You can't let him flood that field with Jupiter's daddy still stuck in there!"

He made no reply. It was then that Remmie took a step backward as her eyes fixated on his chest. Her look of consternation was replaced by one of utter shock.

"What are you...?" started her father. "What are you looking at?" He looked down at his white shirt, half expecting to see a mauve-colored tea stain. When he saw nothing wrong, he repeated, "Remmie, what are you looking at?"

She could find no words. They seemed to vacate her thoughts the way water disappears when poured into the sand of a beach. There, in the center of his chest was a heart glowing in the complete absence of goodness. Remmie mumbled through shaken lips, "Like a rotten pumpkin." Her eyes glazed. "Just like the brown and black of a rotten pumpkin." She took two steps backward not realizing how close she was to the stairs.

"Remmie, no!" he yelled. But she tumbled down the steps of the front porch and spilled out onto the dirt below. Graydon Moon scrambled after his daughter, "Remmie! Remmie, are you alright?" He reached down to help her but she jerked back from him as though repulsed by the touch. In sudden disapproval of her own reaction, she halted.

"I'm alright, Papa." Her eyes fixated on him again. "But Papa, Washington's body. You can't, you can't allow it. Wait, Papa, you didn't tell Mordecai to flood that field did you?"

Words started to emerge from his mouth, but she interrupted. "How could you? How could I have been such a stupid little girl! Papa! These aren't just slaves, they're people. No wonder...no wonder you're heart is all black and guckey...you, you...you've changed! You're not the Papa I once knew."

"Remmie, you've got to understand, I've got a plantation I'm responsible for. Decisions have to be made. That rice has to start right now or we'll miss the growing season."

"Rice? Rice? Do you hear yourself? We're talking about a man down there."

Moon's face toughened. "He's not a man; he's a piece of property. And besides, he's dead."

"If Mother were here, you wouldn't have talked like that! You wouldn't be doing this." She stormed into the house and Fanny chased after her.

Mordecai was standing on the earthen dike, his boots half covered in wet black mud and little bits of rotten reeds. "I said get off that rice field!" He turned towards another slave driver, "Go on, pop the wooden pin out'a that gate lock. Tide's already comin' in. Should fill this field in an hour or two anyway."

The driver walked down the dike towards the wooden door, and pulled a hammer from his belt. With it he pounded upwards against the wooden pin jammed into the gate's locking mechanism. It only took one blow to dislodge the pin. There was two feet of water on the other side of the gate, and when it swung open, the gate slammed into the mud bank on the other side. The torrent of rushing water drowned out the cries of the slaves, still scattered in the area near Washington's body.

Some slaves pulled against others in an attempt to clear the hopeless field. There was nothing any of them could do, and all retreated to the dike. Each mans legs and hands were covered in a mixture of both fresh and dried black mud, the dried mud plainly obvious due to its much lighter color. As the brackish water crept forward towards the body, little Jupiter, still sitting with his back against the scene, began singing.

"No more, my Lawd,
no more, my Lawd,
Lawd, I'll never turn back no more."

The other slaves turned towards him, some sobbing. There was something in Jupiter's voice, something in the way his unblinking eyes gazed off into nothingness, and something about their whole situation that caused all to join in.

"I found in him a restin' place,
and he have made me glad,
No more, my Lawd,
no more, my Lawd,
Lawd, I'll never turn back no more.
Jesus, the man I am looking for,
can you tell me where he's gone?
Go down, go down, among the flower yard, and perhaps you may find him there."

"Mr. Winkles?" said the pigtails.

He looked at her with mist in his eyes. "Yes, little Missy?"

She reached as far around him as she could, and gave him the best hug she knew how.

"Well, thank you, Missy. What was that for?"

"I just thought Jupiter needed a hug right now."

28
A Hurricane of Calabash

Four hundred nautical miles to the southeast, the islands of Spanish Wells, Great Abaco, and Grand Bahama bore the brunt of the storm that had first been seen by explorer Paul du Chaillu as he stood on the coast of Africa. At that time, the storm was just one of nature's after-thoughts, but now wind speeds roared ahead of the fast-mover and tore into the tiny islands, ripping trees from their roots, and pushing an unforgiving wall of water over everything in its path. Villagers living along the lee sides of the storm took the worst of it. Those on the high ground, what there was of it, had a fighting chance.

But back on the tiny Georgian isle of Saint Simons, no alarm bells were sounding on the town streets, for no one knew of the approaching danger. Had they known, they would have fled by boat days earlier, seeking higher ground on the mainland.

The breeze blowing from the east seemed a little out of place, but the Graydon Moon plantation took no notice. In fact, the slaves toiling in the blazing afternoon sun welcomed it.

On the top floor of the plantation house, Remmie lay on her bed. The shock of seeing her father's heart wracked in wickedness overtook her every thought. It was unlike any of the other hearts she had seen, including Mordecai's. They had all been a mix of colors, but what overpowered the reds, blacks, and ochre, was the bright coating of white—an almost fluorescent purity. The purity was like a ship's anchor; it was the righteousness that girded thoughts, actions, passions, and beliefs of the person, and it held steadfast, as long as the person did. Her father's heart, however, looked like a tossed-out and rotted calabash.

What worried Remmie was that, like the calabash, a heart coated in that much wickedness was something not bound for anything past this world. It would be tossed to the side and could perform no further function other than to fertilize the soil. It would decay into nutrients that are once again sucked up into use for another try. Graydon Moon hadn't a chance of being allowed into the Magic Place, but Remmie did not yet know this.

The tide rose, and with it, the height of the waterline inside the rice field. The rising tide acted as a perfect mechanism for flooding rice fields on the Georgia coast. The planted rice seedling is delicate and cannot withstand a heavy flow of water. The slow, almost monotonous, movement of the tide provided the perfect speed at which to bring water onto this slight crop.

The tide comes twice daily; it is relentless in its quest. It knows no bounds, it pays no mind, it trembles for no one. And when it comes, it does not announce its coming, nor wait for an invitation. On Saint Simons and the other 'Golden Isles,' its rise and subsequent fall is six feet or more—six feet of water, six feet of nutrient-rich fluid gold. A spin of both salt and inland river runoff that is as consistent as the rise of the sun, the veiling of night's darkness, and the very presence of a living God who dwells among everything.

The tide knows no spring, nor summer, nor autumn. It is perpetuity in its persistence, in its quest, in its complete un-breakability. And the tide has no feeling, no compassion, and particularly, no patience. When it comes, it comes, and whatever is in its path had best move.

As the cool waters ebbed forward through the gate of the rice field, the body of Washington, faithful father, leader of his clan, confidant, and once-and-for-all-time, a human being who God loved deeply, was dampened, then soaked, then covered with the dark, silt-filled water. It was only an hour before the tide rose to a point at which the body was no longer visible. But even at the tides highest mark, the stump stood erect and peeped just above the water, like the eyes of an alligator lurking just below the surface.

Everyone standing on the dike held hands, gently humming the same solemn chorus. They stood in place and they all knew—the body was there, and Jesus was watching.

29
A Cleaning of Hearts

Up the stairs, Jupiter crept. He had never been inside the plantation house, much less the upstairs. Fanny had sat him down and told him he would now be living in her room. She would take care of him, and be the mother, and father that he no longer had.

At the top of the landing, Jupiter stayed low, almost crawling, and peered through the hand-carved stair-rail posts. Remmie lay across her bed, and was face down, crying.

He went towards her, but dared not enter her room. Instead, he cupped his hands, looked back over his shoulder, and whispered to her.

"Remmie, Remmie."

The school children found themselves once again standing next to Mr. Winkles. This time, they were on the balcony of the plantation house, just outside the bedrooms. The balcony spanned the width of the house. The huge white columns pierced its outer edges and girded the railing—perfectly painted white spindles. The balcony itself was as deep as the porch below, and mirrored the three sets of French doors, one coming off each bedroom.

Mr. Winkles held Lenny's hand on one side, and the pigtail's hand on the other. The rest of the kids circled tightly behind as they tiptoed across the creaking planks.

"Y'all stay quiet now. Y'all stay so, so quiet," he said. "Get real close to me, and follow me over to the window."

The small huddle of people closed in around the window, and crouched low. They could see Remmie on her bed, and Jupiter's head peeking just around the corner.

"Can they hear us?" said Lenny.

Winkles replied in the breath of a whisper, "Not if we stay so, so quiet. Not if we stay so, so quiet." His last sounds trailing off like a man distracted.

Remmie startled, but more from the surprise that Jupiter was there. Her face was red, her eyes wet, and in the pale light of dusk, she looked like a fawn stirring awake in the first light of morning.

"Jupiter, come sit with me."

"I can't, Remmie, I can't." He looked back down the staircase. "Ain't proper. I'll just sit right here and we can talk."

"I saw it," said Remmie.

"What? What did you see?"

"It's my daddy, Jupiter. Oh, it's my daddy! His heart, his heart is filled with...it's filled with bad things."

But Jupiter's facial expression did not change, and to Remmie, it seemed as though her friend was already aware of the fact.

"Well," said Remmie, "how come you...why don't you look surprised?"

The boy fiddled a finger through the hole in the bottom of his shoe. "Remmie, you know I'm your friend, don't you?"

Remmie sat straight up, "Well, yes, of course, but why would you..."

"Remmie, I don't wanna say anything that makes you sad."

"But?"

"I'm sorry, Remmie. I'm truly sorry." He looked back down the stairwell to reassure himself no one was listening. "Your daddy, he's a *slaver*, Remmie." The word shivered out like a snake slithering over his feet.

"Well, Daddy owns slaves, yes, but..."

Jupiter interrupted her. "There's no slaver that is a good person, on the *in-side*."

"Well, that's just awful! I can't believe you'd think my daddy is a..." But the vision of Graydon Moon's heart roared back into the forefront of her mind and she knew he was right.

She sat down on the large circular rug at the foot of the bed. Jupiter's eyes locked on the carpet—he had never seen such a tapestry design. She looked at him but seemed distant, like she was staring over his shoulder into nothing.

"Jupiter," she said, running her finger along the design in the rug, "why do you think we got into the Magic Place?"

"Dunno," he shrugged, "but seems to me like I was being led there. You know? Like when you're walking someplace and your daddy's holding your hand." The thought of his father reared again, but he quickly squelched the lump in his throat.

Out on the balcony, Lenny backed up, and looked like he might sneeze. Winkles put his finger under the boy's nose, and the sneeze retreated.

"Thanks," whispered the boy.

"You're welcome, Meestah Lenny. I sure don't want them to hear us out here."

"Mr. Winkles, they can't really hear us, or see us, can they?" He was no longer asking it as a question.

Winkles once again gazed in through the glass. Lenny shook his head, and wondered if he was right.

"That's what I think too," said Remmie in full agreement. "I keep thinking about it. You and I have been running around together in those woods for as long as I can remember. And I know we always stayed away from the path that led to the still because we thought there was the ghost down there, but we must have run back and forth across that very path without even knowing we were on it. And we never saw any of those things before. And most of that magic path, it's so full of trees that are all jammed up against one another. And that tunnel—I just don't understand, we'd have run right through those spots."

"I've been thinking the same thing. What do you think it means?"

She leaned forward and whispered, "I think it means God wanted us to find that path. I think he's been hiding it." She sat up again. "I don't know why he showed it to us, or why he showed it to us *today*, but it's like my momma always said, he's got his reasons, and it doesn't matter if we know what they are or not."

"So, what should we do?"

"Seems to me, if he showed us that place for a reason, that we've got to figure out what it is, and I think I might know."

"You do?" asked the boy. "What?"

"When I came out of that Magic Place, I could see people's hearts. I can see right inside their heart and tell if they're good or bad."

"Yeah? But what does that mean?"

"It means Jesus is showing me their hearts for a reason."

"But what's that reason?"

Remmie thought a moment. When she turned to gaze out the window, everyone on the porch ducked. "So, here we have this little spot in the woods that is just like heaven, right? And now I can see that some people have bad hearts and some have good, right? It seems to me we should take the bad folks into the Magic Place, so they can get their hearts fixed."

Jupiter sat bolt upright; his eyes and mouth wide.

"Take them in there?" he said. "You mean, take your daddy in there? With his bad heart? And who else, that driver, Mordecai? He's got a bad heart, I know he does. But then what? Is Jesus gonna clean their hearts for them?"

"I don't know, but we have to try."

Outside her window, the wind gusted once, subsided, and gusted again. Had she looked across the vast marsh, and past the far tree line, Remmie would have seen the darkening sky—the first trickle of the coming storm.

30
Jesus Knows No Black Heart

"Mr. Winkles?"

"Yes, sweet pea?"

"Jesus gave Remmie a way to see hearts." She stared at his chest. "So, now they're going to bring the bad-hearted men into the Magic Place? Hmmm, I don't know."

"What bothers you about that, little Missy?" He studied her in an act of almost willing the child to think deeper.

"I never thought about it before now, but I'm not so sure Jesus wants us in heaven with bad hearts."

"Oh no?"

"No. It seems like he wants us to clean them up before they get there. You know, kind of like how my momma doesn't want me to come inside when I've got mud on my shoes."

"Oh, she does? Mud on your shoes, you say. Well goodness, you sure have been thinking about this thing, haven't you?"

She said nothing, but her smile evolved into pride.

"Alright, y'all gather around old Mr. Winkles, and we gonna talk about this thing. The first thing we've got to know is, who here, and y'all can raise your hands, who here doesn't have a single bit of dirt, or darkness, never had any bad thoughts, never said anything mean, never did any wrong to anybody, nor none of that? What, no one? Nobody here has a pure heart, just as pure white as we seen when we were in the Magic Place and Remmie's momma came up?" He surveyed the group. "Hmmm, well, we've got to think about this," he said, scratching his chin whiskers. "Hmm, well, now, this kind of makes a problem for Jesus, doesn't it?"

"Whatdaya mean, Mr. Winkles?" questioned Lenny.

"Well, and y'all don't get scared or nothing when I say this, but, suppose something terrible happens, right here, right now, and all of us sitting up here on this porch die?" Their glances darted back and forth between one another.

"Suppose that happens. What is Jesus supposed to do with us? After all, none of us has a heart that is as white as snow, do we?" He glanced down at the pigtails. "What you think, little Missy?"

The pigtails looked at her feet over slumped shoulders.

"I guess maybe not. I guess maybe Jesus doesn't mind if we come to heaven with dirty hearts."

"You right as rain, Missy, right as rain." Thunder clapped in the distance. "Oooo, well, you right as rain, and I think rain's coming. So anyway, Jesus doesn't mind us coming to heaven with dirt, or sin, or whatever you want to call it, on our hearts." He leaned further into the center of the circle. "Y'all listen real close to what Mr. Winkles has to say. *It ain't our experiences nor any sins we've done that make the person.* Nossirree. It's our *loving actions, thoughts, choices, and hearts.* Those make up the you that are truly you, and that is the heart that Jesus knows. And he doesn't care if it's clean or dirty. He loves you just the same."

"But Mr. Winkles," squeaked the pigtails, "how does Jesus clean our hearts in heaven? I mean, once we get there, and there is dirt in our hearts, he wants to clean them, right? So, he's got to clean them out somehow, right?

"Oooo, you right about that, little Missy, yessirree, just as sure as you're born, you are. And you know what else he has to clean? He's got to clean your face. Little Missy, you got just the littlest bit of dirt on your chin. So, anyhow, y'all all hear what little Miss Pigtails asked? What she's asking about is how Jesus cleans our hearts when we gets to heaven. Well, he does clean our hearts in heaven, sure enough. But, he doesn't have to wait till we get there to get to cleanin'. Nossirree, he don't. See, Jesus has the best cleaner in the whole world. Yessirree, he does."

Lenny piped up, "My momma says the best cleaner is something she calls Clorox."

"Oh, she does? Well now, maybe one day I'll meet her, and she can tell me all about that Clo-rox, Lenny." He ruffled the boy's hair. "Like I was saying, Jesus has this cleaner, and it's called *grace*, and grace is the best..."

The pigtails flopped as the girl's head spun around, "Mr. Winkles?"

"Oh, ah, yes, sweet pea?"

"Grace is right over there," she said, pointing to a little girl on the outer edge of the circle. "She's my friend."

"Well, ain't that special! It's nice to meet you, Miss Grace." The little girl blushed until her cheeks matched her fire-red hair. "But this grace I'm talking about is something else. Yessirree, this grace isn't a person, no. This grace is the best gift God ever came up with, umm-hmm."

"What does it mean?" said Lenny.

"Grace? Oh, grace is kind of like forgiveness, but, it's bigger than that. Grace is the kind of forgiveness that doesn't know any bounds. There has never been any bad thing anybody ever did that grace couldn't handle." The children stared at him as if he were about to perform a magic trick. "Grace washes over us when we do something bad, and that's Jesus' way of saying that we are forgiven. And you don't have to go to heaven to get it either. Jesus gives grace to us any time we need it. And, if I must say, from the looks of some of y'all, Jesus must be mighty busy giving out his grace!" The children laughed.

"How do we get it, Mr. Winkles?" said the pigtails, tugging on his sweater.

He looked down at her like the grandfather he was. "All you have to do is ask him for it, Missy. And he's gonna come into your heart and bring his grace with him."

Most of the ooo's and ah's had subsided when Lenny chimed in, "My momma says Clorox isn't free, though. She has to pay money for it at the grocery store."

"Ha ha!" laughed Winkles. "Yes, I bet she does, Lenny, I bet she does." Then Winkles looked harder at the boy. "Lenny, what else are you thinking right now?"

"I'm still wondering about Remmie, and what her and Jupiter are talking about doing—bringing her daddy and the slave man into the Magic Place." The boy spoke without making eye contact. "If Jesus doesn't care about all that dirt and stuff in their hearts, then why doesn't she take them in there with her?"

"So you're thinking all she has to do is just invite them in? Uh, huh. Anybody else got anything they wanna say?"

"Mr. Winkles?" said the pigtails. "My momma says that if you invite somebody, that doesn't always mean they're coming."

"And your momma is right as rain, yessirree." His hands went wide into the air. "Y'all hear that? We can invite somebody to come with us, to come with us as we're finding Jesus, but that doesn't mean they're going to come."

31
A Storm's First Anger

On the steps of the plantation, Graydon Moon yelled out, "Mordecai! Mordecai! Get over here."

"Yassir," said the slaver under his breath. Then louder, "Yassir, I'm comin'."

Mordecai trotted up toward the base of the steps and instinctively knew to stay on the landing below. He made it a point to never traverse onto the porch without being invited.

"Yassir?"

"Mordecai, shut them up. I don't want to hear any more of their wailing. What's done is done. I want them back to work, and now."

A ruthless gust of wind roared across the far marsh, and into Graydon Moon's face. It tore his hat from his head and sailed it across the yard. The hat rolled to a rest underneath the pair of twin magnolia trees.

"Lordy," said Mordecai, "that there wind blew up on us awful quick."

Moon's gaze would not avert from the darkness forming off the coast. "What? Yes, looks like a storm is coming. And go get my hat. My God man, what do I pay you for? And I want them back to work, you hear me? I don't care; get out the whip if you have to."

Mordecai started to move towards the hat, "Yassir." But he didn't get more than three steps before Moon's next words stopped him cold.

"And don't think for a moment I've forgotten about the mortgage still due on Washington." It was like delivering a sharpened spike into Mordecai's gut.

Mordecai turned back in abrupt fear. "But sir, I, I, I didn't mean for him to die! It was an accident, sir." Graydon Moon stood stoic.

"Sir, I, please, I can't pay the price of that mortgage, I ain't got that kind of money."

"Well," said Moon, with the justified air of the throne, "you should have thought about that before you put a boy into that pit."

"I never knowed the stump would snap back. And, and I never knowed Washington would jump in there like that. A'sides, we had to get that field planted and flooded, and..."

"Your stammering annoys me, annoys me to the quick."

Mordecai wrung his hat in his hands. The hat was so crushed it looked like it had been slept on. In the barn, horses began to stir, apparently in protest of the increasing winds.

"Yassir. Ah, Sir? I hope we can work this out. I shore do like tendin' them slaves fer ya sir. And I promise to do the best job I can, sir."

Graydon Moon glared down at him as a man revolted at the sight of a slug. Mordecai ran forward to retrieve the hat. Then, under the guise of aristocracy, Graydon glided back into his manor home, oblivious to the danger of the approaching storm.

32
A Chariot to Carry Me

A violent gust tore across the marsh. One could almost see the wind as it bent sawgrass in half, moving in waves across the vast marsh. Pine trees in the distance rocked wildly, though just for a few moments. The women slaves in the far cornfield looked up at the contrasting sky—half white with high clouds, half black with others that fired in anger, bearing their gritted teeth against the land below. Like the ocean tide, the wind made no friends, asked no one for directions, yielded to nothing, and did not extend a neighborly hand. Yet somehow, this was a part of nature; unwelcome, but unavoidable should you be in its path.

Lightning rocketed from the leading cloud-bank with a literal roar. One of the women, whose sackcloth was still half filled with dried corn grains from last year's harvest, stared up at the sky, then spoke. "When I'm a little girl, my grand-momma told tale of a storm." Her eyes darted back and forth across the violent sky. She looked down, and sunk another corn seed just beneath the blackish red soil. "She say God's wrath be comin' again. When she was a little girl, she thought that time had done come as a big storm blew up. All she 'members, was wakin' up soaking wet up in the crook of a oak tree, way up high. She say it was the only tree she could see fo' a long, long way. She stayed there some days 'til a red skinned woman climbed up and pulled her outta there. She never done seen what happened to her kin-folk, but she knew...she knew." The woman sunk one seed, shuffled on her knees to the side, and then sunk another. A few moments later, another woman, an older matriarch, started to hum, then sing about a chariot that would one day come to carry me home.

In the parlor, Graydon Moon startled as the wind gust slammed into the walls of the front porch. The force was powerful enough to be felt throughout the house.

"Good Lord," he said. "Even though it isn't the good Lord."

Jupiter and Remmie ran down the wide, semi-circular staircase, but Jupiter stopped at the middle landing. Remmie continued to the bottom of the steps, and then wheeled around.

"Jupiter? What is it?"

The boy stood frozen, lost in concentration.

"Jupiter?" she repeated.

His only response was to nod his head and mumble something not loud enough to hear. Then a wide smile wrapped across his face and his eyes darted back and forth like he was basking in some kind of glory.

Down on the front porch, Mr. Winkles and the children tip-toed across, staying low, and moving toward the wide-open front door.

"Shhhh," said Winkles, "y'all stay quiet, y'all stay sooo quiet."

Lenny stood bolt upright, "Oh, come on, Mr. Winkles. They can't see us, now can they?"

He paid the boy no mind, and continued leading the group towards the door.

"Y'all all get down as we go past this here window." This was an almost impossible feat since the windows along the front porch reached nearly to the floor. The group was completely exposed.

The children ducked low, and some even crawled under the window. "Alright, y'all stay right here, and y'all others tippy-toe up to the door. Peek around the corner and look in there. We got to see what's goin' on inside."

Lenny's hands rest on his hips as he walked past the window, nonplussed at the need to hide from anyone.

"Shhhh," said Mr. Winkles as he pushed his hat back and wiped his brow. "Let's hear what they're saying."

33
Forgiveness

Remmie ran up the stairs back towards the boy. "Jupiter?" she yelled. "Jupiter?" It was the second yell, a frantic sort of yell, that startled him from his daze.

"What? What?" he said, as he half-sat, half-collapsed onto the landing.

"What happened? You weren't answering me. You're scaring me. What's wrong?"

"Wrong? Oh...nothin's wrong. I'm fine. I'm just fine. It was my daddy! He appeared to me, right here. I saw my daddy just then."

"You what? You mean, here, on the staircase?"

"No, yes. Well, kind of," he said. "I mean, it wasn't like he was standing here on the stairs with us or nothing. It was like, all of a sudden, I could just see him somehow, and he was talking to me."

"What did he say?"

The boy propped his elbows on his knees, and leaned his hands against the side of his face. He relived the conversation, yet some parts were difficult to recall. "He said...he said there ain't nobody that Jesus doesn't love." He shut his eyes tight and placed his hands over them. "He said Jesus loves everybody, no matter what they've done. My daddy told me that he forgave that slaver, Mordecai, even after all the bad stuff he did to him. He forgave him." Jupiter looked up at Remmie. "I hate Mordecai, Remmie, I hate him! He's so mean. He killed my daddy!"

"Hush now," said Remmie, as she sat down and placed her arm around him. "Shhhh. Quiet now. Let's just sit here a bit."

Jupiter spoke more quietly, "But I hate him, Remmie. I do."

"I understand, but..."

"You don't! You don't understand. My daddy's dead because of him. And worse than that, he's a mean man, he's always been a mean man. He's always hitting folks, and hurting them."

Remmie startled.

Jupiter bore a gaze into her that seemed to go straight through. "He likes it, Remmie. Mordecai likes hurting folks."

"Oh my God. I didn't...I didn't know."

"That's because your daddy doesn't let you around when he allows that slaver be mean to us."

"My father knows?"

Jupiter stared down at the swirling pattern on the oak stair where he was seated, then ran his fingers across it. "Your father knows, he knows. I've seen him. He'll be standing right there when it's happening. Terrible things, Remmie, terrible things."

Anger welled inside of her, but it was more than anger, it was a feeling far worse—betrayal. Anger could be overcome, but betrayal carried with it a far more egregious sense of wrong; the feeling one gets with labored breathing, and a fear in the belly. To Remmie, it felt like wearing the cloak of the devil.

Out on the porch, Mr. Winkles turned towards the children.

Lenny put his hand on the grandfather's shoulder with the gentleness of a child. "That slaver man. He was mean to you?"

Winkles looked at him, not willing to say too much. He replied in a hushed tone, trying to speak past the lump in his throat. "He was a mean man. He was mean to lots'a folks. He did bad things, bad, bad, things."

Little Missy edged closer and leaned her head on his shoulder. She and Lenny seemed to be the only two who knew who Winkles really was. In the tenderness of the moment, the little pigtails leaned up and kissed him on the cheek. The grandfather could hold back his emotions no longer. He wrapped his arms around them and squeezed tight. Although he remained quiet, his body heaved in gentle succession, up then down. He sniffled once, and then looked at the two of them. "I'm supposed to be the story teller here. I'm supposed to be helping y'all, but it's y'all that's helping me."

"It's okay to cry, Mr. Winkles," said the pigtails. "Even my daddy told me so. It's okay."

"You know, y'all is the bestest story telling group I ever had."

"You're the best story teller we've ever had," said Lenny.

"Really?" said the old man.

"Just as sure as you're born," replied Lenny.

Winkles hugged at the boy again and laughed. "Okay, so we got more to talk about with this here thing, don't we?"

"What else, Mr. Winkles?" said a boy wearing a baseball cap.

"Well, we've got to talk about what Jupiter's daddy is telling him."

"What does it mean?" said the pigtails.

"Yeah, which part?" said Lenny.

"Jupiter's daddy is telling him that Jesus loves everybody, right? But, it ain't just that, y'all already know that. He's saying he loves everybody no matter what they've done." He studied their eyes. "*Why* do y'all think Jupiter's daddy is saying that to Jupiter right now?"

The children exchanged glances.

Winkles read their looks, "Jupiter's daddy said he forgave the slaver man, Mordecai. He wants Jupiter to forgive him too."

"You mean forgive him, even after he got Mr. Washington killed, and Jupiter's supposed to just forget all about all the other mean stuff he did?"

"Forgive, yes. Forget? No." He paused. "Sometimes, folks do some terrible, terrible things to us. Jesus can remember what they've done wrong but he forgives them anyway. And for us, if we don't forgive that person, we're gonna carry around that wrong-doing with us the rest of our days. What you gotta ask yourself is, *how long are you gonna carry this stuff around with you*? See, Jesus wants us to forgive them folks that do wrong to us. He's gonna forgive them, so he wants us to forgive them too. That doesn't mean we've got to forget what they did. After all, Jesus himself doesn't forget. And, how could we? Ain't no magic that can make us forget things that happened to us, even things that happened a long, long time ago. But we don't wanna carry that stuff around with us any more. It's kind'a like carrying around an old suitcase full of mud. Ain't doing anybody any good to carry that around with them. You've got to let it go."

34
The Search for Lost Souls

Remmie ran out the front door with Jupiter in tow. But as their feet hit the painted floorboards of the porch, a gust of wind struck them head-on. It was strong enough to push Jupiter back against the outside wall of the house. A roaring sound rose, then fell again. It was the sound of wind ripping across the marsh and scissoring the blades of sawgrass against one another.

Both children startled at the force of the gust. Jupiter began to run forward, but stopped. His head cocked to the side and he looked about himself.

"What?" said Remmie, "Is a bumble bee buzzing around your head?"

Jupiter held his hand up, signaling her to be quiet.

You got to hurry. That storm, it's more than a squall, son. There ain't much time. It was the voice of his father.

"Remmie!" said Jupiter, "Something's wrong. That storm comin' over yonder, it's not right. I'm tellin' you, it not right!"

"It's bad?" She wasn't really questioning him.

"It's real, real bad. We've got to hurry."

They leapt off the porch in a bound, and began their frantic search for two men that they considered 'lost souls.'

"Papa?" yelled Remmie. "Papa!" But the howling of the soon-to-be hurricane-force winds overpowered her meek voice. Under the roaring wind, slave men fled the job site at the new rice field, ignoring the drivers. They ran towards the row of shacks hidden behind a berm of young pine trees—hidden because Gravdon Moon didn't want to look upon them. The shacks lea
one another in groups of four, separated by a span of
Men ran with elbows cocked in front of them, guarding against the

buffeting wind; and all knew, this storm was different, this storm was violent, and this storm, worst of all, was true.

Fear rose in their hearts but did nothing to slow their run. They were determined to get to their wives and children. Each man broke off in succession and angled into their shack through slatted wooden doors, and ran into the arms of frantic mothers with children clung to their necks, stomachs, and legs. The wind slowed, and then gusted again, each time becoming stronger. The actual hurricane-force winds were yet to arrive, and no one on the plantation was prepared for the coming cacophony—two-hundred-mile-per-hour winds that would push a wall of water capable of engulfing them all.

Remmie and Jupiter became frantic, and the more frantic they became, the direr their situation seemed. Remmie's screams for her father were equaled by Jupiter whose voice seemed to roar. His vocals sounded like they came from the bowels of a freight train's coal oven. And while Remmie yelled for her papa, Jupiter yelled for Mordecai, a man he hated down to the depths of his soul. But one thing was clear, their world seemed to be coming to an end, and the only thing left to do was to grab what souls they could, and head for the Magic Place.

"Mr. Winkles!" screamed Lenny over the slamming wind. "I'm scared!"

"It'll be fine, Lenny, it'll be fine! We'll be alright! All y'all listen up," he bellowed. "Y'all stay with old Mr. Winkles, and everything's gonna be alright. We'll be back under them oak trees out in front of the library back home in just a bit." He crouched low and held a hand on his straw hat, lest it blow away in the wind. As they stood in front of the plantation house, he waved his hands signaling the children to circle about him. Then he took to one knee, his hat buckling under the thrust of the wind.

"Y'all listen close, now, you hear?" His old voice tired as it yelled and his finger wagged at them. "Every last one of you is gonna be fine. Ain't nothing gonna happen when you're with Mr. Winkles. Y'all understand?" The wind rocketed past 80-miles-per-hour, and a pine tree snapped half way up its height, then crashed to the ground, narrowly missing the barn.

The children nodded at him, yet one little girl standing next to the pigtails began to cry. "I want my momma," she said.

Winkles shuffled on his knees over to her and held her in his arms. She buried her head in his neck. "It's gonna be alright, now. You just hold Mr. Winkles round the neck, and you'll see. Nothing's gonna happen to you when you're with me. And soon, you're gonna be back under them great big oak trees down by the pier, and your momma's gonna be right there, okay?" The girl seemed to settle, and he put her back on her own feet.

35
Droplets of Liquid Life

Remmie and Jupiter still could not find either Remmie's father or the slave driver, Mordecai. The rain began a steady rip, flying in horizontally. Jupiter grabbed Remmie by the shoulder, however, he wasn't listening to what she was yelling. He was again listening to the voice of his father. *Take all our folks into the Magic Place, son. Get all our folks, and head them into the Magic Place. Ain't gonna be easy, and I can't help none, but you try.*

"But Papa! I'm supposed to find Mordecai and Remmie's daddy! I thought you said I've got to find them!"

Do as I say, now. There's something you got to do. Do as I say.

Jupiter squinted against the rain pelting his eyes. His mind raced. "Remmie!" he yelled straight into her ear this time. "Daddy says to get all these folks into the Magic Place!"

"What? But we can't, we have to get my papa and Mordecai and try to save them." But it was no use. Jupiter was already headed into the first of several shacks.

Remmie ran after him and her dress flailed about her legs and became soaked in the drenching rain. It wasn't until she bolted into the first shack that she realize she had never been inside the living quarters of any slave, including Jupiter's. It's not that she'd never wanted to, it was that she'd never been allowed.

She looked around the tiny, single room, and was at once ashamed. The shack was nothing more than a decrepit wooden shell atop dirt. There were no belongings or furniture to speak of aside from a few stumps cut from pine to serve as seats. Built into the rear wall was a section of stacked stones, packed in mud that served as a fire pit. A wooden spit stretched across the pit and was supported on both sides by thick-hewn branches that formed a fork on each side for the spit to rest. One lonely metal pot hung from the spit by a piece of tattered vine, woven from what appeared to be muscadine. It was the sight of the muscadine vine that triggered Remmie's anger. It reminded her of the entrance to the Magic Place—a place of goodness and purity. Yet here she stood, her feet on dusty, Georgia sandhill and dirt. Remmie now believed her father's heart was as hard as the packed soil beneath her.

It was a combination of the terror of the coming storm, the deplorable conditions of the shack, the fear in the eyes of the slave women—all huddled around little Jupiter—along with the white-hot light pouring from their hearts, that set Remmie's emotions into a whirlwind. How could her father allow people so pure, so decent, to live this way, while she lived in a glorious mansion that sat not 200 yards away? Her world was crashing around her, and her head spun.

The gusts of wind buffeted into the rickety shack and shook the walls. The dust from dry, years-old pine tar shimmered down from above. In one long blast of wind, the house leaned as though a team of horses were pulling against it. The three slave women in the house grouped together in a terrified huddled mass. They surrounded a grandmotherly woman, and screamed at the sight of the buckling walls.

Jupiter looked back through the open doorway, having noticed the degree to which the structure was leaning, and began yelling. "We've got to go! Y'all all follow me." But the women were paralyzed with fear.

The central beam holding the roof overhead snapped, unleashing an ungodly crack. Jupiter leapt into the air and crashed down on the three women, tackling them just as the building collapsed. Remmie, who had been standing in the open doorway, was the only one not hit by the falling debris. She was shocked into a stupor at what she'd just seen, and fear wracked her psyche.

She yelled, "Jupiter, no!" and to her great surprise, his voice returned from underneath the pile.

He was yelling to the women pinned underneath the roof debris with him. "It's gonna be alright! It's gonna be alright! Remmie, help get this stuff off us! We've got to get out of here."

Remmie fought her mind free from its frozen oblivion and yanked at the debris, but most of it was pinned down by the weight of the massive beam. She pulled and pulled, but could not dislodge it. She stood up with frantic eyes. "I can't! I can't move it!" She glared into the pile of debris, and although she could not see past the mash of wood, pine boughs and dirt, she could see the distinct glow of warm white light pouring from the hearts trapped beneath. "Jupiter! Are you alright?" she yelled.

"Yes," came the muffled reply, "but we can't get out. Go get some folks to help get this off of us!"

Remmie ran without thought. She yelled into the next shack, then the next, but to no avail—the shacks were empty—there was no one to hear her words.

With terror in her heart, she ran back to the collapsed structure and began another frantic pull against the heavy beam. But her strength was no match for its weight.

"Jupiter! I can't find anybody." Fear roared up through her throat. "I can't make it move!" She pulled and pulled against the stubborn beam. It was then that the sounds of the roaring wind settled, and became silent. Remmie spun around and looked across the marsh, towards the distant pine trees, expecting to see them standing motionless. But they continued rocking in anger as the wind's violence tore at everything in its grasp.

The storm was not gone; it was simply that she could no longer hear it. Even the feel of the wind that had pushed so forcefully against her long dress was no longer there. To Remmie, it felt like she was now in a dream, or watching herself from above. She began to move in slow motion—the stillness and utter quiet were surreal. It was in this new silence that she first heard the voice. It was not a voice that produced sounds typical of a person; there was something different about it. It came first as a whisper, like the sound of something trickling off the feathers of a hummingbird. The sound surrounded her and penetrated her heart. In the distance, trees were being uprooted and tossed aside—enormous oaks and sapling pines all facing the same horrific turmoil. But she felt and heard none of it.

Her eyes lost focus and she began to see movement. From the corners of her vision, tiny droplets of light shot in different directions. They flopped and moved like jelly, and in their whimsy, they looked like glowing raindrops that had forgotten the force of gravity, and began a rhythmic dance. The randomness of their swirling produced a dizzying spectacle and Remmie began to feel nauseous. But once she stopped her eyes from following their individual motion, and instead began to stare through it, a shape started to form in front of her. At first, the shape was unidentifiable, but slowly the droplets of light began to congregate in a tightly confined space. The more that sloshed into the space, the brighter the light from the space became. As each droplet entered, its wild movements yielded, and more peaceful ones began.

Remmie was mesmerized by the whole thing. The harmonic sound escalated in volume, and with each new droplet, the volume increased. The congregation of droplets was forming into the shape of a person.

More and more droplets radiated towards it. They moved randomly at first, but then began a steady path towards their destination. The shape of the person solidified further, but before Remmie could see the face, she began to comprehend an unexplained understanding that these droplets of light were living beings—not trapped inside the shape, but free.

The gift she had been given in the Magic Place, the ability to see hearts, was what gave her the skill to understand what she was seeing now. She didn't know how and she didn't know why, but as she stared at each light droplet, she entered into the confident knowledge that these droplets were people, people she knew—not in her day to day life, but nonetheless, she knew them in total.

She knew their names, the minute details of their facial features, the way their hair curled, what their thoughts were, who they were as people, and most importantly, she could feel their love—love for her, love for one another, but most of all, love for the person that was forming in front of her eyes.

When the last droplet of light entered, the shape solidified into that of a man. His features came into sharp focus. He was an

average looking man in pants of rough canvas, and wore the long
sleeved shirt of a workman—not entirely different from the garb
worn by slaves. His jet-black hair was long and wavy and his thick
beard seemed to melt into his high cheekbones. His feet were clad
in nothing but thin sandals, handmade of delicate tan-colored
leather, and his black eyes were calming, familiar.

But it was when he held up his hands that she first saw the
marks. On each hand, in the center of the palm, was a deep,
circular scar. She put her hands in his and freely let tears roll down
her cheeks. The man smiled and a glow from the happy lights that
dwelt within him eased out.

"Try it now," he said. The voice was calming and familiar.

In her daze Remmie could not process rational thought. The
man smiled once more and repeated, "Try it now."

Remmie turned and looked at the heavy roof debris pinning
Jupiter and the others. "It's too heavy. I can't lift it."

He simply nodded. Remmie bent down and pulled against the
heavy beam. Its weight rose without strain and the screaming from
underneath the debris quieted. Jupiter and the slave women
scurried out from underneath, and stood. Just then Remmie began
to strain against the sudden load—its weight having increased a
hundred fold. The sheer mass of the debris yanked against her
hand, demanding to be released. As she let go, it flung downward
and slammed into the ground letting out a shrill shriek as though it
were a living object. All winced against the pierce of the shriek, and
no one knew what to think.

When Remmie turned around, the man was gone and the howl
of the screaming wind was upon them once more. This time, debris
flew at them from across the marsh and pelted into their bodies.
Remmie grabbed at the women and yelled the words, "Come on,
follow me!"

Though none could hear her, they all knew what she meant.
The group huddled together into a jumbled run, dodging flying
debris. When they got to the edge of the tree line, they found the
rest of the slaves, all pulling against one another in a panic.

Remmie pounded her hand onto several of the men's shoulders
to get their attention, and yelled at them to follow. But in their

panic they exploded into all directions, running without purpose and scattering away from her. Remmie screamed and screamed but they were gone. She and Jupiter held one another and braced against the torrential winds and horizontal rain.

Then, above the storm's roar, they heard another huge cracking sound. Turning in the direction of the plantation house, they saw the structure buckle, shift off its foundation, and crack into two massive pieces. The upper floor ripped off and fell behind the lower, taking the enormous white columns with it. It buckled as it hit the ground and was caught like an umbrella in an enormous wind gust which sent the roof section into a shattering roll towards a group of bent over magnolia trees.

"Remmie!" yelled Jupiter as he pointed in the direction of the house. "It's your daddy! That's your daddy!"

"And, Mordecai!" yelled back Remmie. They broke into a sprint towards the men.

When they got there, the two men were massed together, looking at the splintered house in horror.

"Papa! We've got to go! You've got to follow me!" She wrenched her father's arm and tugged him towards the wood-line where she could access the path to the Magic Place. But no sooner had they crossed into the trees did she look back to find Jupiter still standing next to Mordecai. The man was crumpled in a ball with Jupiter hovering over him and yelling.

Remmie released her father's grip and ran back.

"You come with me right now!" screamed Jupiter.

The man was frozen in fear, but responded, "No, no, I can't. Ain't nowheres to go no-how!" he yelled back.

Graydon Moon ran up behind them and grabbed at Remmie, but she ripped herself free.

"Get up! I can save you. I can save you!" screamed Jupiter.

Graydon was dumbfounded beyond comprehension as he watched the slave boy trying to save the very slave driver who was responsible for his father's death.

"Remmie, come on!" said Graydon Moon, but she would not budge.

Mordecai stared at the boy, bewildered, and blinked his eyes against the stinging rain. Jupiter crouched next to him and placed his hands on the man's stubbled face. It was the most tender thing Remmie had ever seen.

Through a choking voice, Mordecai said, "I ain't worth savin'. I ain't worth savin'. The things I done! It's too late for me now."

But Jupiter was having none of it. "You've done wrong! You've done terrible wrong. It's your fault my daddy is dead! But if there's one thing my daddy taught me, it's that there's nobody that can't be saved."

The man stared at him through incredulous eyes; his face fully drenched with rain and unable to process rational thought.

"You ask to be forgiven. You ask to be forgiven right now!" Jupiter yelled, but Mordecai was motionless. With that, Jupiter closed his own eyes and yelled into the storm, "God! I forgive this here man for what he's done! And God, you forgive him too!"

Mordecai looked ashen and could not speak. Jupiter reared his arm back then struck the man full across the side of his head, and yelled at him. "Say it! Say it! Say you're sorry!"

Graydon Moon lunged towards the boy with an open hand raised with the full intent of striking. But Remmie jumped in front of him with a fierceness in her face that even her father had never seen.

Mordecai was shocked into submission—the raging storm, the fear of his own death, being struck violently by a slave, a slave boy whose father he'd been responsible for killing—it was all overwhelming and blood rushed to his face. He looked at Graydon Moon almost seeking permission, but pushed past all that and looked back to Jupiter. "I don't know how," he cried.

"Everybody knows how to ask to be forgiven. Call his name. Call to him and he'll hear."

"Jesus," said Mordecai, but he looked as if a serpent might rush out of his mouth and turn against him. "Jesus, I done a lot'ta wrong in my time, a lot'ta wrong. You know what all I done. I shouldn't have done none of it. I shouldn't have been so evil. I done wrong, and I need your help."

"Now ask him!" screamed Jupiter as he braced himself against a shock of wind. "Ask him to come into your heart."

"I can't! I can't," he said, shaking his head hard. "There's nothing but filth in my heart." He looked around himself with wild eyes, "Boy! We gotta get outta here! This storm, it's gonna kill us!"

Jupiter reared back once again and slapped Mordecai so hard that rainwater blasted off his face—the droplets shattered into the wind and were gone. For an instant, Mordecai's face was dry.

"He's seen hearts more dirty than yours. And besides, ain't nowhere to go! Ain't nowhere we're gonna escape this storm. We're all gonna die and you know it! Now ask him before its too late."

"Remmie!" yelled her father, "come on! Hurry, we can't stay here!"

"No, Papa!" she yelled. "You're next!"

This time Mordecai let the words sink into him. He clasped his hands together and yelled, "Jesus! Jesus, come into my heart. Come into my heart and clean it all out." With that he erupted into tears that were made invisible by the pelting of the rain.

"Papa!" yelled Remmie as she grabbed his arms, "now you! Now you! You ask for forgiveness! Ask Jesus into your heart." But the man simply hoisted Remmie from around the waist and ran towards the tree line with her in tow. Jupiter and Mordecai followed close behind.

"Where can we go?" Graydon Moon yelled.

"Follow us!" said Jupiter. But Remmie couldn't peel her eyes from her father's face.

"Papa, now you listen to me! You ask for forgiveness!"

"I'm not an evil man," he retorted as the group ran.

Remmie, however, knew differently.

36
The Devil

Mr. Winkles led the rattled children through the forest, past the old still, and back onto the trail leading to the Magic Place. Inside the buffer of trees that lined the path, all was calm. There was no wind, no pelting rain, nor any flying debris. The children began to release their grips off of one another, and look around with amazed eyes. Above them, through the tips of the tall trees, crystal clear sunlight shone through. They may as well have been a world away, and in fact, they were.

"Everybody okay?" said Mr. Winkles. "Now I told you you'd be just fine as long as you're with old Mr. Winkles."

"Mr. Winkles?" said Lenny from his usual place right beneath the man.

"Yes, Lenny?"

"I wasn't scared none."

"Oh, you wasn't? Well, that's just fine, Lenny."

The pigtails broke in, "But you said we'd be back under the big oak trees and our mommas would be there. But we're not."

"You're right as rain, little Missy. I did say that. But, I wanted to talk to y'all about everything that just happened back yonder."

"That was Jesus," she said. Her voice was resolute. "All those little lights floating in the air. That made up Jesus, didn't it?"

All the children looked at her, then at Mr. Winkles.

"Yessum," he said. "Yessum, that was Jesus."

"Mr. Winkles?" said Lenny, who then looked up at the skylight. "What were all those little lights? They were so beautiful, and, and, it was like, they were alive."

"You're right about that, Meestah Lenny. You're right about that. Those lights? Well, they're something special alright. Those lights ain't just little glowin' drops of water. Those lights are *souls*."

He let that sink in for a moment. "Human souls. All of those souls dwell with the son. They're living inside of him, like all of y'all are gonna do one day when it's your turn to go to heaven. Like I did when it was my time. He made us all. We dwell in him and he dwells in us. What more wonderful place to be but in the Son?"

"Oh, Mr. Winkles," spouted Lenny, "your time hasn't come to go to heaven yet. You're still here."

The old man looked at the boy and only smiled. He then turned his attention to the pigtails whose shoulders betrayed a slight trembling.

"Now little Missy, you still scared sweet pea? I promise, it's gonna be all alright."

She looked around and held her tears in check. "I...I know, Mr. Winkles. But I got scared back there. It scared me."

"Which scared you?"

"When those ladies and Jupiter were trapped under there. It scared me. I thought they were going to die."

"I know, sweet pea, I know." His voice was soothing.

"But," she continued, "that wasn't the worst part."

"It wasn't?"

"No. It was when it screamed that I got really scared."

Winkles stared at the girl. He had hoped to avoid this discussion.

"When what screamed?" asked Lenny as he pushed his glasses further up his nose.

"She's talking about that shrieking sound that came out after the roof collapsed. After Remmie lifted that heavy beam up, she had to drop it back down once the women and Jupiter got out. Did y'all hear that shrieking sound? It came right then when she dropped that big old wood beam. Sounded like an evil thing, that's for sure."

"What evil thing?" said Lenny.

Winkles took off his hat and his nervous hands fiddled with it. "The *most* evil thing," he said, staring at the ground. "It was the devil himself." He looked at each child. "Y'all got to understand. The devil will use whatever he can to try and do bad things, or try and help folks make bad choices. Y'all all listen to old Mr. Winkles. Y'all are going to be growing up soon, and all along the way, he's gonna put things in front of you; bad things, things that'll tempt you. He's hoping you'll take those things. He enjoys getting folks to turn to wickedness."

"But won't Jesus be there to protect us?" said the pigtails.

"Oh, he'll be there alright, yessum. He'll be there. But Jesus needs your help in this here thing too. Yessirree." The old man took to one knee. "See, Jesus loves every one of y'all. And he loves you so much, he doesn't want to control every little thing you do. He wants you to make your own decisions. Wouldn't be any fun if everything you did was controlled, would it? And if y'all think about it, if Jesus or God is controlling lots of stuff y'all do, well, that's kind of like taking the *you* out of you. Know what I mean? If he's controlling you, you wouldn't be able to be yourselves. He loves all of us just the way we are. So Jesus lets all of us make our own choices. He lets all of y'all decide what you are going to do. And that's just part of how he loves on you."

"But the devil is..." started Lenny.

"The devil is trying to get in the way of that love," interrupted Winkles. "He's gonna try to get in the way of it, and get y'all to grow apart from God. Because, if he can separate you from God, you not so strong any more. You ain't a threat any more. And it's easier to get you to do worse stuff." He took a deep breath. "What I'm trying to say is that Jesus is there with you the whole time, but he is going to leave it up to you to make the right choices."

"But," Lenny said in defiance, "doesn't that mean God lets bad things happen to us? I mean, if he lets everyone do what they want, and doesn't stop them when they're going to do something bad...why doesn't he just stop the bad?"

The old grandfather took Lenny and sat him on his knee. "Lenny, if God stops the really bad stuff from happening he'd have to stop anything bad from happening. And you know what that means? That means he'd have to stop every last one of us, right?" He looked across at all the children, then raised his own hand into the air. "Y'all raise your hand if you ever done something bad."

It took a moment, but all hands wandered into the air.

"Yep, that's right. See, to God, there isn't any one sin that's worse than any other sin. So the really big sins are considered by

God to be just the same as the really little ones. Remember when we talked about you missing the airplane by two minutes and somebody else missing it by twenty minutes? But both of you missed it no matter how late you were? It's like that. And I'll tell you another secret. God just loves to have his folks come home to him. Do you all know when folks come home to him? They come home to him when they're in pain."

"Like when they fall down and get a boo-boo?" said the little pigtails.

Winkles chuckled. "Well, yes, little Missy, yes. But, I'm thinking more about when folks are sick or when something bad happens, or when they made the wrong choices and their lives are all messed up. That's a time when they come back to God. They come back because they are needing his help. I don't want y'all to think God wants anything bad to happen to you though. He doesn't. But when something bad does happen, he knows you'll be coming to see him. So, anyhow, these are two reasons God lets things bad happen sometimes. One, he loves you, so he has to let you make your own choices, even if they're bad choices, and two, he loves it when you come home to him." He looked deep into Lenny's eyes. "He loves when his children come home."

37
The Twinkle Winkle Twilight

The small group led by Jupiter ran through the trees with their arms stretched above their heads—a futile attempt to protect themselves from crushing gusts of rain and wind, and flying debris. Dead branches ripped off trees and were hurled in whatever direction the winds would take them. Tree tops of loblolly and long-needle pine thrashed in wild circles. Some snapped and were tossed high into the air. Those that didn't get caught in the tops of neighboring trees crashed to the ground in a cacophonous thunder.

With each blast of wind, hundreds of rock-hard baby pine cones cascaded to the ground in a violent torrent—their weight and razor sharp prickers sliced flesh wherever it could find it.

Graydon Moon was panic-stricken. He held Remmie in a tight grip and ran through the pelting pine cones and debris behind Jupiter. Jupiter turned several times to yell in a desperate attempt to keep the tiny group together. In the ever-changing landscape, he struggled to find his way. Nothing looked the same. The thin trails he and Remmie had taken earlier were covered in all manner of branches, boughs from oaks trees, and dead palmetto leaves that had been torn from their roots.

Remmie's level of panic was escalating as well. She knew if they did not enter the Magic Place, they would all perish. But another thought haunted her—what if when they tried to enter the Magic Place, her father was unable—blocked from entry. She knew he wasn't a believer, not really anyway. She could see it in his heart. She yelled at him repeatedly, but in his fury-filled running, he didn't even hear her.

Another deafening cracking sound pierced their ears. Graydon Moon stopped and looked upwards, but it was too late. The topmost section of a long needle pine tree, about ten feet across, crashed onto them and knocked them both to the ground. Remmie let out a high pitched scream. It was just the right pitch to be heard above the howling winds. Jupiter spun around and ran towards the fray. A pine cone struck him squarely in the face and cut a deep gash underneath his right eye. He yanked the pine branches off of Remmie, who stood. Her father, however, remained dazed. He was fully conscious, but had the wind knocked out of him. Remmie took quick advantage of the moment. "Papa! You have to listen to me! There's no time. You have to ask. You have to ask Jesus into your heart. Do it now!"

Moon looked at his only child and blinked as the rain washed down his face. "Child," he yelled, "I'm a good person..." but she cut him off.

"I can see it! I can see your heart. It's filthy black in there Papa! Listen to me. If you don't ask Jesus into your heart, *where we are going, you cannot follow!*"

The man stared at her but ignored the demand. He stood, grabbed Remmie by the hand, and screamed to Jupiter. "Which way?"

Jupiter ran past the old still with the group in full pursuit. When they came to the entrance of the Magic Place, he turned and grabbed Mordecai by the shirt, and then continued forward. To the others running close behind, it looked as though he had disappeared right in front of their eyes—simply vanished into an invisible thicket.

Remmie and Graydon Moon were next. But as they tried to enter, both were unable. To Remmie it felt as though opposing forces of a strong magnet were repelling her. She leaned into the force, but simply rolled to one side or the other. She remained unable to enter.

Jupiter saw what was happening and knew immediately what the problem was. He was the gate keeper, the port key, the ferry man. He and he alone could act as a guide to bring others into the Magic Place—it was the gift he had been given. As blood streamed down his face from the fresh gash, he positioned his body halfway in the entrance, and stretched out his arm.

"Come on!" Remmie ran into the entrance, yet once inside, her father was no longer holding her hand. Even though Remmie could see him, he could no longer see her. She was in one world, he was in another. Remmie was shaken by the quiet solitude inside the space, yet right in front of her, where her father and the slave women stood, the storm intensified. Remmie yelled but her yelling had no more effect than if she were standing on the surface of the moon and yelling back to earth. Both the women and Graydon Moon gawked at the sight of Jupiter. His body was half in, half out, and they could only see part of him. The women clutched one another and backed away, terrified of the scene. Jupiter jumped out and grabbed them. This time they followed him and disappeared into the entrance. Jupiter re-emerged and once again stood halfway inside the entrance and extended a hand to the plantation owner. He lunged forward but was knocked back to the ground by the magnetic force. He stood and tried again, but simply rolled off to one side and crashed onto the soaking ground.

Jupiter leaned as far out as he could, and then yelled, "Master Moon! Master Moon! Take my hand." But as soon as he yelled these words he began to hear a voice coming from inside the Magic Place. It was the voice of his father. *No one can decide for him, Jupiter. He has to decide for himself.*

Jupiter yelled again at the struggling Graydon Moon who fought the magnetic force in a desperate attempt to enter the one bastion of safety. Another tree snapped and the percussion from the sound blasted into Moon's ears. There wasn't even time to look up before the massive limb of a water oak tree crushed down. The full weight of the limb landed squarely on the man, and he was engulfed by the mass of leaves and branches. There would be no effort made to rescue him—he was gone.

From inside the Magic Place, Jupiter heard a blood curdling, primeval scream. It came from somewhere deep inside of Remmie. It was her voice to be sure, but sounded almost inhuman. She had witnessed the whole thing, and there was nothing she could do about it. Graydon Moon had made his choice—not a choice to go *against* God, but a choice that did not welcome the Son into his heart. When his death occurred, no one inside the Magic Place, the sole sliver of heaven on earth, expected to see the departed Graydon Moon inside its confines. They all stood, and they all knew.

From a hiding spot, Mr. Winkles ran his hand across the scar under his right eye, and then whispered to the children. "I'm sorry y'all had to see that. Everybody okay?"

Lenny was the first to speak. "He doesn't get to heaven, does he?"

"No, Lenny, he doesn't."

"And it's because he was a bad person? Because he owned slaves?"

"Y'all listen to old Mr. Winkles now. Ain't nobody sinned too much that they can't get into heaven. But they've got to be sorry for what they've done and ask Jesus into their heart." He paused a moment. "But even my Master Moon's death had a purpose. He tried hard to get into the only place he thought might be safe against the hurricane. And in his taking up all that extra time, that caused Remmie and Jupiter and all of the slave women to remain standing up near the entrance to the Magic Place for a little while longer."

"But what does that matter?" questioned the pigtails.

"Look over my shoulder and you're going to see."

The children craned their necks and stood on tippy toes. They watched as Jupiter leaned outside the Magic Place once more and yelled at the slave men who were running through the trees in a frantic mass. One after another darted into the entranceway past Jupiter.

"Did you all see?" said Winkles, never having looked at the entrance. Slave men ran past and then went deeper inside.

"So if Remmie and Jupiter hadn't stayed standing up at the entrance, trying to get Master Moon to ask Jesus into his heart, they wouldn't have seen the slave men, and the slave men wouldn't have gotten inside?" said the pigtails.

"That's right, sweet pea. They'd never have seen those men out there if they hadn't been standing where they were for that long. Does that mean anything to you?" He looked at all the faces. "See,

Master Moon's dying isn't a good thing. It's a terrible thing. But God used that terrible thing for good. He didn't want it to happen, but once it did happen, he chose to do something good from it."

Winkles looked down at Lenny who was tugging at his sweater again. "Mr. Winkles? What happens now? What happens to all these people that made it here into heaven?"

"Well, little man, this place is a place of being free. Heaven means a lot of different things to a lot of different people. Y'all remember the legend I told you about when we first sat down together? The legend of those slaves, the kin-folk of the Gullah people that walked across the water all the way back to their home in Africa? Well, in the morning these slaves are going to do just that, yessirree. Just as sure as you're born. They're going to do it. And me and Remmie? I mean, ah, *Jupiter* and Remmie, well they're going to go on up to the big heaven and be with Jesus. Jupiter also will get to be with his daddy. And he doesn't know it, but his momma is still alive and living down in New Orleans. She'll be up to be with them in heaven accordingly. And Remmie is gonna spend her time in heaven with her momma. Y'all already saw her. And they're all going to have the *grandest* time. Do y'all understand the wonderment, joy, merriment and magic now? Like I told ya, way deep down south, in the windey, warm, waterway, lies the Magic Place. And if you can just believe in it, the Magic Place lives on."

"Mr. Winkles," squeaked Missy, "what's your first name?"

She looked into his eyes, and just as she caught her own reflection in them, he said, "I think you already know."

When the children looked next, they were again seated criss-cross applesauce under the massive oak trees down by the pier on Saint Simons Island. And Mr. Winkles? He was nowhere to be seen.

~~~

Thank you for reading! I have a gift for you.

Dear Reader,

I hope you enjoyed *Twinkle*. I have to tell you, I really love the character of Mr. Winkle. Many readers wrote me asking, "What was the inspiration for him?" And in truth, he more or less materialized in front of my minds eye. I've always had a place in my heart for Uncle Remus, and Mr. Winkle is an embodiment of those great Joel Chandler Harris stories. The character of Uncle Remus was so endearing. I wanted to capture some of that here.

When I wrote *Twinkle*, I got many letters from readers thanking me for the book. Some had opinions about how I interpreted the story of salvation, while others were more interested in giving thanks for spreading the word about God. As an author, I love feedback.

Candidly, you're the reason I wrote *Twinkle*. So tell me what you liked, what you loved, even what you hated. I'd love to hear from you. You can write me at Nathan@NathanAGoodman.com and visit me on the web at NathanAGoodman.com.

Finally, I need to ask a favor. If you're so inclined, I'd love for you to put your rating of *Twinkle* on the website where you purchased the book. Loved it, hated it—I'd just enjoy your feedback. Reviews can be tough to come by these days, and you, the reader, have the power to make or break a book. If you have the time, I would greatly appreciate it.

Thank you so much for reading *Twinkle* and for spending time with me.

To get a free copy of my bestselling thriller novel, go to NathanAGoodman.com/fourteen/

A word of warning though, that one is not for the feint of heart….

In gratitude,
Nathan Goodman

Other works by Nathan A. Goodman:
Bestseller, *The Fourteenth Protocol*, an FBI thriller. Get a free copy at NathanAGoodman.com/fourteen/

Nathan A. Goodman is a husband and father of two daughters and lives in the Atlanta, Georgia, area. He attends Buckhead Church.

Interested in more from the author? Sign up for notifications of upcoming works at NathanAGoodman.com/email.

www.ingramcontent.com/pod-product-compliance
Lightning Source LLC
Chambersburg PA
CBHW071313200626
46813CB00015B/1850